D. P. Sanford

Eunice Somers

A Learner in Life's School

D. P. Sanford

Eunice Somers
A Learner in Life's School

ISBN/EAN: 9783337056445

Printed in Europe, USA, Canada, Australia, Japan

Cover: Foto ©Andreas Hilbeck / pixelio.de

More available books at **www.hansebooks.com**

EUNICE SOMERS

A LEARNER IN LIFE'S SCHOOL

BY THE AUTHOR OF

"THE YOUNG LAYMEN," "THE ROSEDALE BOOKS," "UNDER THE SKY-LIGHT," ETC.

" Pastures lowly, waitings still,
Looks subdued to duty's will ;
Reverent, thoughtful, grave and sweet ;
These to wait on Christ are meet."

NEW-YORK

E. P. DUTTON & COMPANY

713 BROADWAY

1872

ST. JOHNLAND STEREOTYPE FOUNDRY, SUFFOLK CO., N. Y.

CONTENTS.

CHAPTERS	PAGE
I. CONFLICTING DUTIES	5
II. AUNT EDITH'S PROPOSAL	15
III. THE IMPORTANT DECISION	27
IV. PLEASANT PROSPECTS	43
V. HOPES FULFILLED	54
VI. HAPPY CHRISTMAS	71
VII. A CLOUD ARISES	83
VIII. THE CLOUDS SHOW THE SILVER LINING	100
IX. RHODA	114
X. LENTEN LESSONS	127
XI. ANXIOUS DAYS	139
XII. A MEMORABLE WEEK	152
XIII. RANNEY	166
XIV. INCIDENTS BY THE WAY	182
XV. PLEASANT THINGS	199
XVI. "SWEET COUNSEL"	214
XVII. HOME AGAIN	225

EUNICE SOMERS.

CHAPTER I.

Conflicting Duties.

"No fruit of cold neglect ;
But goodly purpose gone astray,
Where jealous care can scarce detect
The first divergence of the way."

"ANNEY! *Do* make a little less noise! I can't hear myself think!"

The speaker was a girl, under fourteen, who seemed indeed to be thinking under difficulties. She was pacing up and down the room, carrying a baby brother, balanced in a peculiar manner upon her hip; while with the other hand she held a book, outstretched as far as she could see the words, to be out of reach of the little one, who was

(5)

kicking and squirming in a vain attempt to possess himself of it.

"Ille, illa, illud:" repeated Eunice, conning her declension.

"Le, la, lud,
My horse is stuck in the mud!"

shouted the irrepressible Ranney, behind her, pretending to urge up his stick horse, desperately. The other children laughed merrily, but Eunice was out of all patience. She put the baby down upon the floor, and seized upon the offender in no gentle mood.

"You are a perfect plague!" she cried : "and if you don't let me study in peace, I'll see if I cannot make you!"

"Stop pinching my arm!" returned Ranney, with a grimace. Then hearing his mother's step in the hall without, he suddenly realized that he was very much hurt, and began to cry accordingly; the baby joining in with all his might.

Mrs. Somers opened the door upon this scene of confusion; and, taking up the baby, looked for an explanation.

"Ranney wouldn't let Eunice study a bit,"

said little Bess, when no one else spoke; "and I guess she pinched him a *little*, but I don't believe she meant to!"

Mrs. Somers glanced reproachfully at Eunice.

"You promised to take care of the children, and amuse them while I was out. I thought I had arranged to give you time enough for study this evening, did I not?"

"Yes, mother, but this was an extra lesson," Eunice replied in some confusion.

"An extra lesson?" Mrs. Somers picked up the Latin grammar, which had fallen to the floor, in the strife.

"Then you could not resist the temptation to begin Latin, Eunice?"

"Well, mother, I could do it, I was sure I could, at odd hours: I could have studied a little, just now, as well as not, if Ranney had not been so—provoking!"

The expression might have been a stronger one, had not Eunice perceived that her Aunt Edith had entered the room. This lady was making a brief visit at her sister's home; and it was on her account that Mrs. Somers had done such an unwonted thing as to go out for a walk in the afternoon, and a call upon some old friends.

"I know I am interrupting a whole train of employment, in asking such a thing;" her sister had said, mischievously, "but I don't feel the least compunction; it is a good thing for you to have some one come and interrupt you, once in a while; you would work yourself to death, else, I do believe."

Eunice was struck by this remark, and by the recollection of the unceasing round of cares and labors in which her mother was occupied. So she had joined quite heartily in urging her mother to go out for the afternoon, declaring that she could take care of the baby, and of the other children, as well as not.

So she could have done, undoubtedly; no one could excel Eunice in amusing little folks, when **her** heart was in the matter. It was a lovely autumn afternoon, and she yielded to the request of the young ones to "bring little Walter out of doors, and have a game with them."

All went on well for an hour or so, and Eunice herself was enjoying the romp; when all at once the thought of her contraband Latin lesson flashed upon her mind.

"There! I meant to have learned it this afternoon : I shall have all I can do in my study hour with my History and Philosophy. Now I shall fail: and then Roland will prim up his lips to keep from smiling! Hateful! I wish he would giggle right out, if he feels so much like it!"

The thought of Roland's contempt, real or imagined, was too much for Eunice; she took little Walter into the house, and essayed to do two things at once.

But baby did not relish the change of programme, and she was obliged to walk with him, to amuse him. Then the other children, their play being interrupted, followed her into the house; and we have seen the result.

The parents of Eunice were persons of intelligence and refinement, as well as of sterling worth. Mr. Somers had been for some years in poor health, which had greatly hindered his business; and, in consequence, the family were in straitened circumstances.

It was not from any want of appreciation, on the part of her parents, of the advantages of a liberal education, that Eunice was obliged to study by stealth. She was the eldest child; and though it was at times very difficult for her mother to spare her, nothing but the demands of some unforeseen exigency was ever allowed to interrupt her regular attendance at the village academy.

But Mrs. Somers was obliged to depend a good deal upon her daughter's help out of school hours; and as Eunice was not very strong, she was unwilling to have her take up so many studies as to require much application out of school.

This year the academy had come into the hands of an excellent teacher, a Mr. Hale, who had inspired all his pupils with a new ambition in their studies.

Among other plans, he had formed a class of girls in Latin, which was rather a new thing in the village. Eunice was very anxious to join this class, but her parents had discouraged her from doing so, for the reasons above mentioned.

Roland Wells, the Roland to whom we have heard Eunice allude, was a near neighbor of the Somers family: he attended the academy also, and was in the same classes with Eunice in English studies.

The two were pretty good friends, in general; but Eunice had confided to Roland her earnest wish to enter the Latin class, and to her surprise and chagrin, he had sided with her parents in the matter. Eunice was vexed, and took up the notion that he thought girls were not competent to study Latin successfully; and it was all in vain that Roland protested he had no such thought.

In fact, Eunice had set her heart upon taking up the new study, and in asking *advice*, she had only sought *approval*, as people often do.

Mr. Hale, her teacher, was quite proud of her scholarship and ambition, and was pleased to allow her to join the class conditionally, lending her a book of his own until she should prove

that she could "make time," as she said, to
carry on the study.

Poor Eunice! She had been obliged to make
time, indeed, out of small fragments, to accomplish her purpose. It had seemed to her that
never had there been such a busy time, as
since she began to study Latin. First, Bess
was sick; then it was house-cleaning; and then
came Aunt Edith's visit.

She had been obliged to smuggle her
grammar to the ironing-table with her, and
hide it beneath the pile of towels, napkins, and
such like, which were her share of the ironing:
in consequence, the said towels were apt to be
folded far from straight, and laid aside with
curled edges. More than once, the same
grammar had changed color upon its open
page, from being stationed upon the shelf over
the sink, while Eunice was washing up the tea-
things, in quite too close proximity to the soap-
dish.

I do not think this argued any improper pride
in the scholarly book, but only a just sense of
the fitness of things.

In short, Eunice had not proved, in this busy time, the efficient helper she was capable of being; and her mother felt that the mystery was explained, as she picked up the Latin Grammar. Aunt Edith had observed a good deal, and guessed at more, of the state of things with her favorite niece; and a plan which she had dimly in her mind when she left home, had matured rapidly during her visit.

To return to the time and place at which we introduced Eunice to our readers.

Aunt Edith laid aside her things, and claimed an exclusive right to little Walter, until tea-time. George and Ranney suddenly realized that the bright October afternoon,—Saturday afternoon, too,—was almost gone; and they rushed out-doors for another game.

Bess and little Susy were wonderfully entertained by the nursery rhymes and comical stories which Aunt Edith was telling to little Walter; *of course*, with no thought of any other listeners.

And so it came about that Eunice had full leisure to finish her lesson, and also to think

over the occurrences of the afternoon. These
thoughts made Eunice feel rather disturbed
and uncomfortable. In fact, this state of feeling was by no means new to her; many times,
of late, had she been made uneasy by discover-
ing a 'flaw' in her work; the inevitable
consequence of 'breaking a thread in the loom,'
by overlooking 'present duty.'

"O dear!" sighed the girl, "everything
that I touch seems to go wrong; why must
things pile up so!   I am sure it would have
been almost wicked for me to lose this chance
of beginning Latin, when I do so want to be
fitted for a teacher!   I would work *so* hard;
and do something and be somebody in the
world, if I could only have the chance! But,
just as surely as I set about anything which
seems really worth while, any quantity of teasing little things will turn up to be done! It's
like trying to run a race through a bramble-
patch!"

CHAPTER II.

𝔄unt 𝔈bith's 𝔓roposal.

"Ask His peace to lull to rest
Every tumult of the breast :
Ask His soul-sustaining truth
As the spring-dew of thy youth."

THAT evening, when the sisters chanced to be together for a short time, supposing themselves with no auditor but the baby,—restless little Walter, whose sleepy hour had not yet arrived,—Mrs. Hartwell took the opportunity to broach her scheme.

"Madeline! Suppose you were to lend Eunice to me for this winter? Now don't shake your head and look such a decided negative until you hear all I have to say. I assure you my project is not to be set aside with a nod. The fact is, what with her home

(15)

duties, and her ambition for study, the child is over-working herself; and not only her health, but her spirits and temper are suffering in consequence. I know that you are aware of this to some extent, and that it worries you; but even you cannot see it as I do. Why, the way she has of carrying that heavy child on one side is enough to injure her of itself; it really seems to me that she is growing out of shape."

"That is true," sighed Mrs. Somers, " and I reprove her every time I see it; but Eunice thinks time is entirely wasted in tending baby, unless she can be reading, or doing something else, at the same time."

" I know—I see how it is. As I said, she is full of girlish ambitions, and they seem to me very laudable ones, in their way.

" I know you think it is very naughty of her to be so unwilling to help you with your heavy burdens, and I do not mean to justify her impatience; only excuse me if I suggest, dear sister, that your shoulders are fitted to the burden, by all wifely and maternal instincts, helping you to bear up under it. Her position is very different. To be sure, she ought to love, honor, and succor her parents, but it is natural, too, for her to be forming plans for her own course in life.

"Now if you *could* arrange to spare her to me this winter, I do think it would be the best thing for her. It would give her time to get over this irritated feeling of being thwarted in her ambitions. I can teach her myself in her English branches, and Ransom will, I know, willingly instruct her in Latin.

"I will attend to her clothing, so that she shall be no expense to you at all; and it seems to me that, when you are relieved of her schooling, and other expenses, you can afford to hire a stout young girl to help you with the baby, and so on.

"Now, dear sister, I want you to think seriously of my plan, before you say 'No;' think of it over Sunday, and talk it up with her father.

"Oh! I had almost forgotten to mention a part of my scheme. You must know we have

an excellent teacher of drawing and painting
near us; and if you approve, I would like to
have Eunice take lessons of him. I have
always thought she had a great deal of taste in
that line."

Now it happened that Eunice had come into
the parlor, from which opened the little sewing-
room where her mother and aunt were sitting,
with the intention of offering to take little
Walter; but she had spied a new magazine
upon the table, and, as her brother George
would have said, had "grown to it," unconscious of baby and everything else, until her
attention was recalled to things passing, by
some of her Aunt Edith's words, which reached
her ear.

"If you *could* arrange to spare her"—"English studies" — "Latin" — Eunice overheard
enough to get the drift of her aunt's proposal.
She heard as if in a dream; but suddenly
aroused herself, and slipped out of the room;
too honorable to remain and listen, although
her heart beat quick with eager longing to
know what her mother would reply. As she

closed the door, however, she heard the words'
"Think of it over Sunday."

Eunice sped up into her own little room, and
bolting the door, rushed forward and threw
her arms around a silent figure, exclaiming :

" Oh, Lucilla, you darling! It is *too* good to
think of! It cannot come true ; but, if it
should!—Oh, if mother *should* say yes!"

And who was this favored confidante ?

I fear my readers will form a low opinion of
the good sense of our Eunice, if I confess that
Lucilla, the beloved, was but a doll !

" A girl of nearly fourteen hugging a doll,
and talking to it ; absurd!"

Doubtless ; yet, my wise and worthy friends
of that interesting age, are you never guilty of
an absurdity, in the privacy of your own
room ?

A girl who has a sister, near her own age,
and sympathizing, as a sister should be, needs
no such device ; but, failing this most precious
intimacy, every young maiden craves some
substitute; and it is well for her if the out-
pourings of her heart be not confided to some

more injudicious bosom friend than poor Lucilla !

To apologize in part for this folly of our
friend Eunice, it should be explained, that
Lucilla had been given to her when she was a
little child; and the really beautiful doll was
for a long time the very joy of her heart.

Little Bess, then the creeping baby,—there
was always one at that stage of progress, as it
seemed;—was the unfortunate means of hopelessly maiming the beloved object.

Poor little Eunice's grief was so heartfelt
and touching as to arouse the sympathies of a
friend, who took the severed head, the face
being uninjured, and skilfully adjusted it upon
the form of a pincushion doll, to stand upon
the bureau, in the little mourner's own room.

The relief and delight of the child well repaid
her friend's efforts. Never was a pin allowed
to inflict injury upon her dear Lucilla; and,
from childish caresses and words of endearment,
Eunice had unconsciously gone on to confide
the deeper feelings of her heart, as she grew
older, to this long-time friend.

In fact, she talked to Lucilla as another
would have written in a journal; only far more
volubly and freely.

"But if it should! If father and mother
would let me go!"

How fast the thoughts of the girl flew onward
as she repeated these words! What a vision
of delight flitted before her mind!

"Think of it!" she whispered; "for a
whole winter, perhaps, no baby-tending, no
hard work, but to study as much as I please ;—
and Latin!—and with Uncle Ransom for a
teacher! Wouldn't I get ahead of Master
Roland a notch or two! He should see what
girls can do!"

If Eunice had overheard what her Aunt
Edith had added about lessons in drawing, I
am afraid sweet Lucilla would have been anni-
hilated by an over-vehement caress.

For, to learn drawing; to sketch from na-
ture ;—possibly to paint well,—had ever been
an object far in the dim delightful distance in
Eunice's dreamings. She had, as her aunt had
observed, a natural taste and gift in that direc-

tion; but there had been so little to call it forth, and develope it, that she was only aware of a great love for the beautiful art.

"When I can teach, and earn a good salary, I will learn to draw," was her mental resolve.

As Eunice still stood, with her arms thrown around Lucilla, the voice of little Bess at the door disturbed her excited imaginings.

"Eunie! Let me in! Mamma has been a-wonderin' and wonderin' where you could be, and I guess you'd better go down-stairs!"

Eunice opened the door hastily. "Come, then; I suppose it is time for you all to be washed and put to bed; don't go in there, Bess: come right down, with me!"

"You needn't be so cross," said the little girl; "I don't want to touch anything, only just to look at Lucilla;—*isn't* she pretty? just as pretty as ever!"

"Of course; why not? But she wouldn't be, very long, if you were to have your way. Come, I can't leave you in there!"

And Eunice drew her sister from the room, not very gently, and closed the door.

"You needn't be so cross!" A very truthful observation, and one which Bess had had occasion to make often, of late.

The "crossness" had been all too common, and excuses had been more and more easily rendered, until Eunice had almost ceased to feel them necessary. But this evening, little Bessie's remonstrance was echoed by the conscience of the elder sister; especially when, on going down to her mother, she was met with a wistful look of tenderness which spoke to her very heart.

"Mother would miss me sadly," she thought to herself;—at least, she *ought* to miss me, but I'm afraid I haven't helped her much of late."

The upbraidings of conscience mingling with the tumultuous hopes awakened within the past hour, gave Eunice enough to think of "over Sunday," as her aunt had expressed it.

She lay down to rest that night feeling that she could not wait until Monday to know her fate. But the blessed atmosphere of calm and rest which is breathed on the morning of the Lord's day, in a house whose inmates are trained to its observance, exerted its wonted influence, as Eunice awoke, and prepared to engage in the duties of the day.

It was not alone the habit of a child of a religious household, which controlled her. Young as she was, and careless as she may have appeared to the reader, Eunice had, some months previously to the opening of our story, " with her own mouth ratified and confirmed the promises of her baptism;" and had been admitted to the Table of the Lord. There are those, I well know, who would strongly object to such a step on the part of one so young, and so immature in Christian faith and experience.

Happily for Eunice, her parents and her pastor held other views upon this point. They believed that the child trained from infancy to walk in the road to Zion, with those whose faces were thitherward, was to be encouraged to persevere in that holy walk and way : they would no more have denied the Bread of Life to the earnest desire of the youthful pilgrim, than they would have withheld the " sincere milk of the word " from the need of infancy.

Eunice was in earnest in the wish and purpose to live as a child of God, although many times she sadly failed in this purpose.

Therefore it was that she tried to put aside from her mind the engrossing question of the evening before, and give her attention to the sacred duties of the day.

Opening her Prayer-book, to glance once more at the collect before going to church, Eunice was struck with a new and deeper meaning in the words than she had noticed before.

It was the Twentieth Sunday after Trinity, and the expression which so fixed her attention, was this:

"That we being ready both in body and soul, may cheerfully accomplish those things which Thou commandest, through Jesus Christ our Lord."

"I suppose, after all, these things I have had to do, that vexed me so, were a part of what God commanded; and I have not been doing them cheerfully, I know."

So spoke the conscience of the girl, as she

stood with her book in her hand, musing. Then followed the question, "What is it that has 'hurt' me, and kept me back from my duty?" and the faint consciousness that she had been trying to walk in a path of her own choosing, and not humbly following on in the way marked out for her.

These reflections were deepened by the sermon that morning, which was upon a text taken from the Epistle for the day: "Be ye not unwise, but understanding what the will of the Lord is."

Before the day closed, Eunice found time, in the secret of her own chamber, to repeat the collect humbly and earnestly, praying also for help to understand the will of the Lord, and trying to resolve to be more faithful in her daily and obvious duties, even if it were decided that she should remain at home.

CHAPTER III.

The Important Decision.

" Tinged too her thoughts some show of fair romance,
The fruit of youth, and nursed by various chance."

EFORE the day closed also, the parents of Eunice found time for prayerful thought and counsel upon the question which Mrs. Hartwell had laid before them. It was a matter not unfit for discussion upon the evening of the Lord's Day, for they both felt that not the worldly interests of their child, alone, were involved.

We will not follow the reasoning by which they were brought to the decision that, on the whole, it would be best for Eunice to go with her aunt. Mrs. Hartwell seemed truly glad when she was told; and when the mother added,—"If Eunice herself is willing, and

(27)

pleased to go : you know we have said nothing
to her yet,"—her smile answered that she
feared no objections from Eunice. It was not
until the children had gone to school that the
matter was finally settled; and Eunice found it
hard to fix her thoughts upon her lessons that
morning.

"I *hope*," thought she to herself, "I shall
know how it is to be before another day."

As soon as she returned from school, she
sought her mother, in the hope that some
allusion would be made to the subject of her
impatient thought. Aunt Edith was sitting
with her at work, and the two exchanged
glances as Eunice entered.

"What shall I do now, mother ?"

"Sit down with us a little while, daughter;
we have something to talk to you about;" and
Eunice seated herself, with a fast beating
heart, on a stool at her mother's feet.

Aunt Edith's proposal was then explained
to her at length; the additional charm of the
drawing lessons sufficing to call forth the look
of delighted surprise which her aunt was confi-

dently watching to see. A pause, during which Eunice hid her face in her mother's lap.

"Well, my child," said, Mrs. Somers, fondly stroking her hair, "what do you think of it? Look up and tell us."

"I think auntie is very kind;—and—and, oh, mother! I should *so* like to go, if you can spare me!"

"Oh, we have talked that all over;" interposed Aunt Edith. "Your mother will have all that you cost her for clothing, and so on, to hire help with."

Eunice looked doubtfully at her mother, who met the look with a smile. Mrs. Hartwell had very little idea with how much of turning and refitting, and with how little of actual outlay for new material, the little bodies of that family were clothed.

A speech of little Bessie's had passed into a proverb in the house:—Once, when she was invited to some little festivity, her mamma demurred, because, as she said, "The child had nothing fit to wear." Little Bess exclaimed, excitedly; "Oh, rip, mamma, rip!" She was accustomed to see her wardrobe enlarged by means of *ripping*.

Eunice was thinking that the oft-tried expedient, which had availed to supply many deficiencies of the wardrobe, would not answer as well to pay the wages of a servant.

"I think I shall manage very well, although I shall miss you, darling," said the mother, cheerfully.

"Walter will soon learn to walk, now, and then Bess will help me very much with him; and, as auntie says, I must try to hire more help."

"Then I shall have nothing to do but study; and oh, how I will work at it!—But, Aunt Edith, I thought,—I mean," added Eunice, a little confused, "had you not better send me to school? I shall take so much of your time."

"We will see," said her aunt; "there is an excellent girls' school near us, if you wish to go to it: but you know I am an old hand at teaching, and you could not have a better teacher in Latin than your uncle; and I thought you were just the sort of girl to enjoy studying alone, with the privilege of getting on as fast as you choose."

Eunice smiled, while her eyes sparkled with delight; and her mother saw, with a secret pang, that her choice was made.

"Well!" said Aunt Edith, in her lively way, "do you suppose, Miss Somers, you can accomplish the important business of settling up home affairs for the winter, packing, leave-taking, and so on, and be ready to go home with me by Thursday?"

Eunice started, and involuntarily clasped her mother's hand: "So soon as that!" she exclaimed.

"Why yes, dear child; think what a visit I have made already! I meant to start for home earlier in the week, but I shall wait until Thursday for the pleasure of your company."

"There comes papa, my love; go and tell him what you have decided. And I must be busy now."

Mrs. Somers kissed Eunice fondly, and hastened from the room; for the tears would start at the thought of so long a separation from her eldest-born.

The two days that followed were all too short for what was to be done in them. Eunice had but little time to think of her charming prospects, amid the bustle of preparation for the long sojourn away from home.

She went to school the next morning to explain the state of things to her teacher, and bid good-bye to him and to her school-mates. Mr. Hale, though sorry to part with one of his favorite pupils, appreciated the advantages she expected to enjoy, and was heartily glad for her.

"I shall expect you to sketch the old Academy for me, when you return," said he, "and write an essay in Latin, at the foot of your sketch, upon the advantages of education!"

The scholars had an additional five minutes of recess granted, in consideration of all they had to say in parting with their young friend; —envying her the delightful prospect of a winter in Holmeford, and protesting how much they should miss her.

"Eunie, there is one little bit of work which you must find time for, before you go away; I mean, to take up those bulbs in the garden;—papa is so busy, since he has been feeling better, that he will have no time to attend to it, and I am afraid George would injure them."

"And my precious mother thinks she will have no time for gardening when her 'right-hand man' is gone!" rejoined Eunice, playfully. "Well, I had better set about it now, then; but how warm it seems, to be taking up plants! The sun is really hot to-day."

"Yes, but we cannot expect such weather many hours longer; we may have a frost any day now;—and we must not lose our dahlias, and other pretty things: we want all the brightness we can have about our little home."

"It will always be bright while *you* are within it!" said Eunice, giving her mother a hug, and turning away to find her garden-hat with something like a tear in her eye. With all her bright anticipations, she began to realize that she should miss her mother.

She was very busy, with her sleeves rolled
3

up, and her trowel in her hand, when she heard a step on the walk, and glancing up, saw Roland Wells close beside her.

The home of the Somers' family was next to the more pretentious mansion and grounds of Mr. Wells, and their pleasant little garden had the benefit of a hedge of raspberry and other bushes with which he had partly enclosed his place.

Eunice met Roland's good-humored smile rather shyly; she was conscious of having been rather uncharitable in her feelings towards him of late.

"I was working in the garden too," said Roland, "when mother called me to run over with this plate of wafers for *your* mother; please excuse the absence of my jacket; and will *you* be so kind as to carry them in? I am afraid of meeting your city friends, you know!"

Eunice complied with this request, and soon returned with the plate, and her mother's thanks.

"Those made me think of your birthday parties, when you were a little fellow, Roland;

do you remember? Your mother always baked wafers for us, because we children thought them so curious, and so nice, too!"

"I suppose you will forget all about those old times now," said Roland; "so you are really going to Holmeford, for all winter!"

"I expect to; wont you be glad to have one girl less in the Latin class?"

"Why, Eunice, what can have given you that strange idea? I am sure I am glad to have any of the girls study it, only"—

"Well, only *what?*" said Eunice, in a slightly defiant tone.

"Why, you know what you told me about the reasons why your father and mother wanted you to put it off; and I thought perhaps, if I were in your place, and my father so poorly, I should feel as if other duties came first.

"But there! Of course I don't know anything about girls' work, and I had no business to give advice. I don't wonder you were vexed, but pray forgive a fellow, before you go away; let us part friends!"

Eunice could not resist his frank, good-tempered appeal; all her ill-nature melted away.

"I don't think I have anything to forgive," she said; "I suspect I have been dreadfully cross; and may-be you were right about the advice.

"But now that father and mother think best for me to go, and I am to have nothing to do but study, you'll wish me good luck, won't you?"

"That I will, with all my heart! I hope you will be ready to teach, by the end of the winter; and perhaps I may be one of your scholars, one of these days; who knows?"

"What nonsense!" responded Eunice, laughing merrily. "But you know I *do* want to be able to teach, as soon as I am old enough, and earn money to help them all at home!"

Roland replied to this with a look of real sympathy, for he understood and secretly admired the spirit and ambition of his young school-mate; and, with a hasty shake of the hand, they parted warm friends as ever.

Wednesday evening had come, and Mrs. Somers was busy, packing, in her daughter's room.

The wardrobe which lay around, to be disposed of in the trunk, was by no means what young girls in general would have thought suitable for a visit to a large town, with such society as Holmeford boasted. The mother would gladly have added to it; but her slender purse obliged her to be content with her sister's assurance that she would see that her charge was suitably dressed.

Little Bess, with her quick eye, noticed the deficiency, and anxiously asked if "Eunie did not want some new frocks, to go to Holmeford?"

"Oh, I guess I shall get along!" replied Eunice, cheerfully. In truth she was not given to much anxiety on the subject of dress. As one of her young companions, who had a girl's usual love for pretty adornings, was wont to remark :—"Eunice Somers would as lief be dressed in a coffee-sack, with two holes for her arms, as any other way, if she might but have

all the books she wanted!"   But this was putting the case *rather* strongly.

"Can you make room for this old friend,
mother?" said Eunice, drawing Lucilla forward
upon the bureau.

"My *dear* child! Why should you want to
take that heavy thing? Do you suppose your
Aunt Edith has no pincushions? Or," added
her mother, suddenly remembering with what
care this relic of her childhood had been kept
in its place,—"or do you really love the old
dollie, yet?"

"Well, if I do," said Eunice, "it is quite
time for me to put away such childish things, I
suppose.

"Bess, would you like to have Lucilla for
yours, to keep in your room?"

"Oh, oh!" screamed the child, dancing about
the floor, "*will* you give her to me to keep in
my room, where Susy and I sleep? I'll love
her just as much as you do, Ennie!—But
you'll miss her, won't you, sister? 'cause you
talk to her sometimes."

Eunice blushed, wondering how the little puss

had discovered that fact. She covered her confusion with the remark: "I fancy I shall miss others at home besides Lucilla!"

Here George entered, with an embarrassed look, and placed a little paper in his sister's hand.

"Will you take this, Eunice, to remember me by? It isn't very nice; but I had no more money!" And George made his exit, speedily.

Eunice opened the paper and found a little emery basket, which had probably taken all her brother's scanty supply of spending money.

"Isn't that just like George, mother?" she said, regarding the little gift lovingly.

"Yes," was the reply; "our dear old blundering boy has a warm heart!"

Again Eunice's conscience smote her at the recollection of how much oftener she had evinced impatience at his blunders and clumsiness, than she had responded to his boyish affection.

Presently Ranney came in, also with a parcel in his hand, of small proportions, and curiously done up.

"Here's something for Eunice to take to

Holmeford, mother; will you put it in her
trunk?"

"Is it to remember you by, Ranney?" asked
Eunice, with some surprise.

"Yes," said the child, but his eyes danced
with fun and mischief as he spoke.

"Let me open it, mother," said Eunice, half
suspecting a trick.

"No, no! Don't open it till you get to Aunt
Edith's; I don't want you to!"

"Well, I will not; mother will tuck it in a
safe corner: is it anything that will break?"

But in the mean time the parcel was opening
itself. The young rogue had not securely
adjusted his string, and after a little tussle with
his envelope, out walked a huge beetle, over
Eunice's clean linen.

"Oh!" screamed Eunice, who had a great
dislike to all the creeping things of the earth,
"take the ugly thing away, quick! Ranney
Somers! are you trying to make me *hate* you?"

Ranney was almost convulsed with merriment
at the sudden appearance of his unwelcome
gift; but as Eunice said this, in a passionate

tone, he tried hard to check himself, and there was a half pleading, half frightened look in his eyes, as they met hers, which the sister felt, and had cause to remember, afterward.

The little boy left the room, carrying his beetle, and shaking with laughter still, in spite of himself, at the remembrance of the fun.

Eunice heard her mother sigh, and said petulantly, "It does seem as if that child was always on the watch to tease and provoke me!"

"You judge him harshly, my daughter; and you have no patience with his provoking ways. He is full of life and mischief, I know, but he is not nearly as wicked as you seem to think."

"Not wicked exactly, mother, but, — well, perhaps it is a good thing for Ranney that I am going away!" A better impulse moved Eunice to add: "I will try to be less easily provoked when I come back!"

The mother said no more until she had finished packing the trunk, which was nearly done.

Then she left the room, and returned in a

moment with a little trinket in her hand;—a tiny gold cross, with a slender elastic cord attached, which she put around her daughter's neck.

"I do not give you this as an ornament, my child; I would rather you would not wear it in sight. But I want it to remind you of my parting caution and advice:

"Remember, my Eunice, that the follower of Christ cannot escape the cross.

> "There are briers besetting *every* path,
>   That call for patient care:
>   There is a cross in every lot,
>   And an earnest need for prayer."

"Do not forget your Christian vows, in your new home. Keep your armor bright, and watch unto prayer!"

A loving kiss spoke the 'Amen' to these words, and Eunice was left alone, holding her mother's gift, and gazing upon it with tearful eyes.

CHAPTER IV.

𝔓leasant 𝔓rospects.

"All that appeared was suitable to one
 Whose fancy had a thousand fields to skim :
 To expectations, spreading with wild growth,
 And hope, that kept with me her plighted troth."

A T an early hour on Thursday, our travellers were fairly on their way. As Eunice bade good-bye to the dear ones at home, she realized, as she had not done before, how much she should miss them, and how strange it would seem to be away from them all; for this was to be her first long absence from home. But the sadness of parting was soon forgotten in the excitement of the journey, and bright anticipations of the pleasures of her new home.

Eunice had never been a dozen miles from

home before, so that a journey of nearly a
hundred miles by rail was in itself a great
pleasure; and Aunt Edith was in a lively mood,
and pointed out to her everything worth noticing by the way.

Eunice had not seen her uncle since she was
a little child, and scarcely remembered him;
the other members of her aunt's household
she had never seen; and, as she drew near the
end of the journey, she began to feel that she
was to appear among strangers. She knew
that Mr. Hartwell stood high in his profession
as a lawyer, and held some public offices in
Holmeford; and in this anxious hour it just
occurred to her to wonder whether he would
quite like his wife's arrangements, and whether
he would really be willing to give up a portion
of his time to hearing her recitations; rather
a small business for him, as she now fully realized. She was therefore greatly relieved
when, on reaching her aunt's home, a tall,
pleasant looking gentleman met them in the
hall.

"You have stolen a march upon me," said

he, greeting his wife; "I should have met you at the depôt, if you had written that you would come to-day."

Then turning to Eunice, he added:

"So this is our young niece; our *daughter* for this winter! Welcome home, my dear! You and I are to have famous times in the pursuit of knowledge, I expect."

The fatherly kiss which accompanied these words made Eunice feel quite at home, and at her ease.

Aunt Edith had not acted unadvisedly in her undertaking. Indeed, her first plan had been to send Eunice to school, while with them; but her husband had suggested that they could easily guide her in her studies, and could more carefully watch over her health under such an arrangement.

Eunice was just the age of one of the two, their only children, whom this uncle and aunt had lost by death a few years previously. Doubtless, a thought of the delight with which they would have watched over their own daughter's pursuits, added tenderness to the interest which they took in their young niece. Though without children of her own, Aunt Edith was at the head of quite a household.

Two sisters of Mr. Hartwell were among its members; these claimed to be introduced to Eunice as "Aunt Mildred," and "Aunt Dora."

The former was a widow lady, considerably older than her brother, and quite an invalid. "Aunt Dora" still retained the name of Hartwell; and also, to some extent, her youthful good looks.

Then there was a young relative of Aunt Edith's, and, consequently, a sort of cousin of her own, who boarded with the family, enjoying all the privileges of a home. This individual presented himself as " Cousin Dick ;" and, after dinner, took upon himself the duty of amusing his young cousin through the evening ; watching her, meantime, as Aunt Dora suggested, " to find out on what points she would be most susceptible of teasing."

The remainder of the week was to be devoted to getting settled in the new home, seeing a little of the town, and doing some shopping.

So Eunice's friends decided for her, at break-fast the next morning. At the same time there was some consultation as to the disposal of her time afterward.

Eunice scarcely knew herself in this novel position; the youngest of a family circle, and the object of general attention and solicitude; she who from early childhood, had been called upon to think for others.

"I shall be obliged to appoint your recitation hour with me directly after dinner, my dear," said her uncle: "rather late, I know; but of course you can prepare your lesson in the morning, at your study hour."

He then inquired particularly how far she was advanced in her studies; and told her aunt that he thought she had better study Algebra also, with him, as well as her much desired Latin.

Eunice's eyes sparkled.

'You would like it then, my dear? Very well, I am sure I shall enjoy teaching such an eager pupil."

With her Aunt Edith, Eunice was to read

history, and review some of her previous studies, as time permitted.

Mr. Hartwell promised to see the drawing teacher, Mr. Neville, and secure a place for Eunice, in one of his classes, at once.

"And what shall *I* do?" said Aunt Mildred. "I think if our dear girl would like to spend an hour occasionally in an old woman's room, I can teach her something in nice needle-work, and fancy-work: what do you say, my dear?"

Eunice was not over fond of sewing, and was no proficient with her needle. But conscious how much more useful she might be at home if she knew a little more of this branch of feminine work, she answered:

"Thank you, Aunt Mildred; I am afraid you will find me a very dull scholar in that line, but I should like to learn to sew neatly, if you will take the trouble to teach me."

The reply, which was quite sincere, gratified Mrs. Ellett, very much.

"And I think," she continued, "I shall claim you as my companion when I ride out; this will relieve sister Dora, when she does not care to go; and I can make the drives pleasant for you, I hope, though I am not able to go very far."

Eunice was not obliged to reason herself into accepting this proposition with thanks.

"I don't see as there is anything that I can do in behalf of my cousin," said Dick; "unless I can tease her a little, by way of keeping her awake in the evenings; or unless she will show herself at 'Putnam & Mills' establishment; where I shall be happy to wait upon her!

"And where I ought to be at this present moment," he added, glancing at his watch, and springing from his seat.

"I thought you were feeling more at leisure than usual," said Aunt Edith, laughing. "If you go to the store now, like a good boy, you shall have the pleasure of waiting upon your young cousin, in the course of the morning."

As to Aunt Dora, she had already assigned herself her part, in private council with her sister-in-law; and she began operations energetically that very morning, in order, as she said, "to make the dear child presentable before Sunday."

4

Little as Eunice cared about dress, in general, she was delighted with the novelty of the shopping expedition; and could not help feeling some interest in the progress of the pretty street-suit, which was cut and fitted, before they returned home, and to which Aunt Dora and Aunt Edith devoted their afternoon.

Eunice wished to help; but as it was a very pleasant afternoon, Mrs. Ellett was going out for a drive, and claimed her promised company when the carriage appeared. Then, when she returned, there was the pleasant duty of writing home, to be performed.

"Oh, mother, I am so happy!" This was the commencement of her letter. Then followed a glowing account of the journey; of the kindness of her Uncle Ransom, and of his sisters. "And Cousin Dick, as he says I am to call him: Aunt Edith says you will know who he is, though I did not;—he is real kind, too; and *so* funny!"

Then came a description of the wonders of the town, so far as they had come under the writer's observation: and after affectionate messages to all at home, Eunice added this postscript, at the bottom of the letter: "I do not see where *the cross* can be, dear mother ; but I will try not to forget what you said."

Another rather exciting day, among these new scenes, and new friends; and then came the day of rest once more.

It seemed to Eunice as if at least a month had passed since she sat in her little room at home, studying the Collect, on the morning of the last Lord's Day.

Arrayed in her new suit, which Miss Dora had exerted herself to finish ; and having undergone the inspection of that lady, and received a kiss, and the sentence: "You will do nicely!" Eunice escaped to her own room to avoid the bantering of her Cousin Dick, and collect her thoughts before going to the house of God. From habit she opened her Prayer-book, and read over the Collect and Epistle for the day ; although she would be missed from the class at the dear church at home. From habit, also, and a blessed habit this,—she strove to fix in her mind the importance of the words she read :

"And serve Thee with a quiet mind."

Eunice felt conscious that this did not describe her service of the Master, during the past few days; had she, indeed, thought much of serving Him? Had not her mind and heart been quite occupied with herself,—and her new pleasures? With a penitent heart she whispered again the words of the Collect.

Then came the Epistle; and as she glanced over it, Eunice drew forth the little cross from its concealment, and kissed it; murmuring, "Dear mother!"

For here was the full description of that armor which she was charged to keep bright; and her mother's very expression: "Watching unto prayer." Reading it over thoughtfully, Eunice wished she could recall the postscript to her letter, written the day after her arrival; how childish it seemed to her, now.

For she felt truly that she might find her cross in the conflict with spiritual foes, while trying to keep her heart right with God, as much when all without was bright and smooth, as when "flesh and blood" hindered her in the.

Christian course. A few moments spent in prayer, and then the sound of church-going bells was heard.

Eunice walked with her Cousin Dick, on the way to church. The latter was but little accustomed to curb his mirthful spirits, from respect to the holy day: yet there was something in the manner of the young girl by his side which restrained the playful jest, more than once, when on his lips: was it the gleam of the Christian armor, burnished by those few moments of real devotion, which checked the careless youth? If so, Eunice was unconscious of the influence she was exerting. A real home feeling came over her, as the service began, soon after they had taken their places in church, and she remembered that at the same hour the dear ones at home were listening to the same words.

When services were over for the day, her uncle, who had observed with pleasure her serious deportment, lent her an interesting and profitable book to read; and so pleasantly passed the first Sunday away from home.

CHAPTER V.

Hopes Fulfilled.

" Beware, beware !
There's hidden danger lurking round,
  In those great books, that easy chair,
This pleasant room, that garden ground
  In the pure, cultivated life
Which seems all duty, yet may be
  But a fair fence to keep the strife
Of a rude world from vexing thee !"

RS. HARTWELL proposed a longer vacation to her niece, but was amused by the eagerness with which she begged to begin her studies at once.

There was a pleasant library, opening from the parlor ; Mr. Hartwell's study, when he had occasion for such a room at home, but his office up-town generally monopolized him, except in the hours of relaxation.

In this pleasant room Eunice was to study,

(54)

to her heart's content, with none to disturb her.

Her uncle laughingly deposited her in his own arm-chair, before leaving for his office on Monday morning, telling her he should "expect her to justify her claim to such an honorable situation."

Eunice found the studies very pleasant; difficulties vanished before her uncle's lucid explanations, at that delightful recitation hour, after dinner; and she could perceive that she was in a fair way to make rapid progress.

The chief trouble her aunt encountered was in making her leave off at the proper time, and take necessary exercise and recreation. She was obliged to go in and "stir up her nest," as she expressed it, very determinedly, morning after morning.

"Just this one example more, please, Auntie!" Eunice would plead; or, "*Do* let me go over this verb once more, to make sure of it for uncle!"

At length her friends were obliged to limit the hours of study, strictly; forbidding Eunice to study more than four hours a day. This her uncle declared was quite enough for such a pale-faced little body.

The drawing lessons began before the first week closed, and Eunice was perfectly charmed with this new pursuit.

Mr. Neville was equally delighted with his pupil, declaring to Mr. Hartwell, after Eunice had taken a few lessons, that she was "a born artist," and that "it would have been a sin to neglect such talent."

It needed an occasional mild reminder from Mrs. Ellett, to keep Eunice from neglecting the sewing lessons, which were excused entirely on the two "drawing days" of the week.

Yet this hour was usually a very pleasant one, spent in the gentle old lady's room ; and Eunice really felt grateful to her for the exceeding pains she took to make her an accomplished needle-woman.

She did not fail to inform her mother of this, among her other advantages, in the frequent letters which were sent on their way to the quiet little home, in Mansfield.

LETTER FROM MRS. SOMERS TO EUNICE.

MANSFIELD, *Nov.* 20, ——.

" *My Beloved Daughter :*   .

"Another of your bright, happy letters has just arrived, and been eagerly read; would you like to hear the comments of each of the household?

" 'Father' read, with a smile all over his face, and laid the letter down with the words : 'Blessings on the child! I am thankful she is doing so well!'

" Then George : 'My! How jolly! I wish I could see that panorama!'

"Ranuey heard you through, and mused : ' I wonder if she'd let *me* go to ride with her, in that nice carriage, if I were there!'

" Truth compels me to add that this was said in a tone of doubt.

"Bessie says, characteristically, 'Oh how I *wish* I could see Eunie in that pretty hat, and nice new suit! I know she looks *just* as pretty!'

"I tell you this with not much fear of arousing your vanity, or of sending you to the looking-glass, to verify Bessie's fond assertion.

"Little Sue says wonderingly, 'Where *is* Eunie? How can she speak in dis paper?'

"And Baby repeats your name from the lips of the others, lovingly, as if he remembered you.

"Then Roland came in, and the letter was read to him; for which we received his thanks, and the remark: 'I am *so* glad Eunice is so happy, and has such a nice chance to get on!'

"'And what did mother say?' you ask. Nothing, audibly; but she said something, down deep in her heart; and it was an earnest prayer that our God will have my child in His holy keeping; making these precious opportunities a real blessing to her, and enabling her to consecrate all her talents to His service!

"Remember, my dear child, I pray you, that you have need to be watchful; your enemies do not sleep, though all seems bright and calm.

"Remember and use the prayer of our Litany: 'In all time of our prosperity, Good Lord, deliver us!'

"Do not feel anxious about me, dear. My strength has held out wonderfully, and papa is unusually well, for him, which makes all things lighter.

"I miss you, of course ; but I am very glad to spare you to such advantages as you are enjoying.

"Tell dear Aunt Edith, and your kind uncle, and other friends, that I thank them, continually, for their kindness to you.

"A most loving good-night, from

"YOUR MOTHER."

Such letters as this the busy burdened mother found time to write frequently ; and they were, as Eunice expressed it, "like ballast to the ship ;"—the little craft which was scudding onward so gayly before helpful breezes.

Ballast of some sort was needed, to keep the head and heart in the right place, in this novel and charming state of things.

"Miss Somers, this will be quite enough of this preliminary work ; I will have you begin studying from casts, with the next lesson, if you please."

A bright smile answering him to his satisfaction, Mr. Neville went on :

"I shall be happy to lend you casts to study
at home, if you choose : as you tell me you have
only this winter to spend here, we must be
getting on as fast as we can."

This proposal of her drawing-teacher gave
Eunice a delightfulexcuse for spending an hour
or two more each day in the library.

The circle whose solicitude centered about
the gentle intelligent girl, began to devise new
ways and means to tempt her out more, for
exercise and diversion.

"I wish she had some young companions,"
said Miss Dora ; "it cannot be very interesting
for her to go about with us old folks !"

"Humph !" ejaculated Dick, who happened to
be in the room, awaiting his dinner.

"Oh ! I beg your pardon, Mr. North ! You
are young and lively enough, certainly, if you
choose to devote yourself to the entertainment
of so young a damsel ; but then, you know, you
are not at home, except occasionally in the
evenings."

"The eldest of the Merritt children is about Eunice's age;" suggested Mrs. Hartwell; "and there are the Hill girls, we might invite them here to get acquainted."

"Now, my respected cousin, you surprise me by your want of discrimination!" quoth Dick. "Whatever the age of the Merritt girl, she is a mere child to Eunice, in her tastes and ways; and those young Hills, with their silly prattle and giggle;—pray don't bore the poor child by associating her with them! They are as unlike her as possible."

"That is true," said Miss Dora; "if Eunice were to grow up in this place, I suppose it would be her duty to cultivate the society of young people of her own age, and do her part towards improving it; but as she is only here for a time, we need not take pains to introduce her to such as would be distasteful."

"I believe I will speak to Frances Lynde, and ask leave to introduce Eunice to her," said Dick.

"Miss Lynde! Why Dick, you are quite as far out of the way as I was, in another direction,"

said Miss Hartwell; "Miss Lynde is a young
lady in society; rather beyond a school-girl of
fourteen."

"Yes," said Dick, "but she has a very winning way with younger girls; there is a set of
them who think all the world of her; she has
them in a sort of Bible class, I believe. And
she would be interested in Eunice, I know; at
any rate, she would take pains to gratify her if
I asked the favor; you know she is a sort of
cousin of mine, on the other side!" supple-
mented Dick, noticing the mischievous glances
exchanged by the ladies.

"Very well; I wish you success in bringing
about the acquaintance;" said Mrs. Hartwell;
"I am sure it would be a very pleasant one for
Eunice!"

"My good cousin," said Dick North, at
dinner, a few evenings after, "I bespeak the
pleasure of your company for this evening, if
you are not otherwise engaged; I have promised
my friend, Miss Lynde, to take you around to
spend an evening with her, at some time; and

this will be a glorious evening for the walk: what say you?"

"Do you mean the Miss Lynde who sings in the choir, and teaches in the Sunday-school, at St. James'?" asked Eunice.

"And is foremost in every other good and pious work! Yes; the very same; do you know her already?"

"No, except by her sweet face; but I should so like to hear her speak!"

"Very well; go with me, and we will hope to persuade her to afford you that gratification!" said Dick, laughingly, with a side glance at Mrs Hartwell.

"Am I to excuse the recitation this evening?" asked Mr. Hartwell.

"Oh, uncle! no, indeed! That is, not if cousin Dick will wait for me; I should be sorry to lose my lessons!"

"Oh, I will wait, by all means; I am quite at your service, Miss Eunice!"

Eunice hardly knew whether to feel teased or obliged by his deference. But she had fully decided, by the end of the evening; which, as she told her aunt, was "one of the pleasantest she ever spent in her life!"

Frances Lynde was really as lovely in character as Eunice had fancied her. She was highly accomplished, too; and played and sang for her guests, to the great delight of both.

On her part, she was very much pleased with Eunice,—"Took to her at once," as Dick expressed it, and seemed to find much pleasure in drawing her out of her reserve. Some allusion was made to the Sunday-school:

"Your scholars are about my age, are they not, Miss Lynde?" Eunice asked.

"Yes," was the reply; "that is the first and only class I ever taught. They were little girls when I began, three years ago, but they have grown up, suddenly, on my hands.

"I have felt as if they ought to be in the Bible Class, or, at least, have a more experienced teacher; but they do not want to leave me, and Mr. Robertson says I must keep the class, by all means, and adapt their studies to their capacity."

As Eunice still kept her eyes upon her face,

with an asking look, Miss Lynde added, "How would you like to join my girls; as you and I are determined to be good friends?"

"Oh, I should like to *so* much!" replied Eunice; "I miss the Sunday-school; but I did not know as it would be best for me to join a class, only for the winter; and then, I didn't care so much about it, among strangers, you know."

"Well then, I shall look for you on Sunday;" returned Miss Lynde; "and, by the way, I know you love flowers; how would you like to walk out with me, to-morrow? I have an errand to one of our largest green-houses. You do not study on Saturday, do you?"

"Indeed, Frances, it is my belief that she would study, or draw, every day and every night, if allowed. But I know her aunt will give you full license to drag her out-doors whenever you can."

"Then I shall certainly call for you, at two," said Miss Lynde, merrily; "and you must be sure to wear clogs, or over-shoes, or something to protect your feet; for we go off the sidewalks to reach Kelly's."

5

"I will," said Eunice ; "I am used to walking in the country, you must remember."

This allusion brought up the subject of
Eunice's home, about which her new friend
asked questions with so much interest, that
Eunice found herself telling 'all about' each of
the children, as to one who was far from being
a stranger.

"That dear little Ranney!" exclaimed
Frances : "your uncle's namesake, I suppose ?
—I should like to see him! I had just such a
little brother once ; as full of life and fun as he
could be! It was so amusing to watch his
pranks, they seemed to be just the overflowing
of health and spirits! You can imagine how
we missed him, when he was taken away, can
you not ?"

Eunice assented ; wondering to herself if
Miss Frances was ever so impatient with her
darling little brother, as she had been with
Ranney.

The next day was pleasant, and the walk to
the greenhouse was accomplished, Eunice be-

coming more and more charmed with her new friend. ·

I wish our young ladies knew how much good they might do, and what warmly attached and grateful life-friends they might often make, by a friendly notice of girls, perhaps five or six years younger than themselves.

Frances Lynde was like an elder sister to the girls of her class in Sunday-school; and Eunice felt that she could well understand the glances of admiring love which greeted her, as she took her place among them.

Some of the members of this class were very interesting girls; they gave Eunice a cordial welcome, by their manner; and promised to prove very pleasant acquaintances for her.

The subject of the lesson for the class was a familiar one to Eunice; the Collect, Epistle and Gospel for the day; the same which, as we have seen, she was accustomed to prepare at home.

Miss Lynde studied the lesson diligently herself, before she appeared among her young sisters in the faith, as their instructress. ·

The Sunday on which Eunice joined the class was the Second in Advent, so that the special topic of the day's lesson was the study of the Holy Scriptures.

Very earnestly did the young teacher seek to press home this subject, to the members of her class.

"Let each of us ask herself, dear girls, whether we do ' in *such* wise, hear, read, mark, and learn' the Scriptures of truth? Nothing else can nourish our souls; all the choicest learning of this world is as ' chaff to the wheat,' compared with the Word of God.

"I want to be very earnest on this point, because I know you all go to school, or are engaged in various studies; and you are surrounded, at other hours, by attractive and interesting books; and there is much danger lest you be tempted to feed your minds upon these entirely, and so neglect to feed upon and inwardly digest the words of eternal life."

"Does she mean that for me alone?" thought Eunice; "how could she know how many times I have forgotten to read my Bible ?"

Miss Lynde did not know, of course; nor did she mean to apply her words to Eunice, more than to the others; except that in the moment of speaking she remembered how Dick had described her eager application to study.

But her words were well-timed; and sank into the heart of one of her hearers, at least.

Some of Miss Lynde's scholars called to see Eunice, during the week, and invited her to visit them.

One sentiment they had in common, which gave them the aid of something to talk about, in getting acquainted; that was their admiration for Miss Lynde.

The girls seemed to feel themselves bound to enlighten the new-comer respecting the praiseworthy qualities of their friend and teacher, but Eunice secretly felt quite sure that they did not appreciate and love her as she did already!

One of these callers was the very Rhoda Merritt, whom the ladies of the family had

passed over as too childish to be a companion
for Eunice. She was backward, in some re-
spects, and very shy. But she seemed to take
a great fancy to Eunice, and evidently wished
to attach herself to her as a friend.

Eunice did not at first reciprocate this feeling,
and was rather disposed to repulse Rhoda's
advances. A thought of the way in which
Frances Lynde had treated *her*, checked this
impulse, and moved her to respond cordially to
Rhoda's urgent request that she would " come
to see her, very soon, and spend the afternoon."

CHAPTER VI.

Happy Christmas.

"Now to the Lord sing praises,
    All you within this place;
And with true love and brotherhood
    Each other now embrace.
This holytide of Christmas
    All others doth deface."

HRISTMAS was near; and Eunice had now no lack of enticements to win her from too close study.

The parish of St. James was a small one struggling to grow with the growth of population, in the outskirts of the town.

There were two other churches, within reasonable distance, which would have afforded Mr. Hartwell's family the advantages only to be enjoyed in communion with an old, firmly established parish; but, knowing that the new church was much needed in the neighborhood, they had deemed it their duty to cast in their lot with the young parish, and give it their help and support.

As Christmas approached, the few workers of St. James' found their hands full; and Eunice could not but enter into the spirit of her Aunt Edith, and Miss Dora, who were among the most active in preparing for the Christmas Tree for the children, and in decorating the church.

Perhaps the meetings for work were more attractive to Eunice from the fact that her friend Miss Lynde was always present.

The Lyndes had joined themselves to St. James' from the same motives which influenced the Hartwells; and Frances, with her rich voice, her fine taste, and her true devotion, was a treasure to the pastor; a real helper in his work.

Eunice had another delightful occupation, during these weeks of Advent. Mrs. Ellett proposed that she should make up a Christmas box to send home.

The good lady had a double motive in this

proposition: the wish to keep up the interest of her pupil in sewing; and a desire to reach, in this delicate way, and minister to the needy family, of whose real situation she had learned a good deal in her talks with Eunice; drawing her own inferences, for the girl had quite too much of her father and mother's spirit, to complain, or consciously acknowledge their poverty.

"Now Eunice, dear; let us put our heads together, and see how many nice useful little things we can get into your box, before it must be sent off.

"I will find you materials for your work; but the children, and your mother too, will think so much more of anything you make for them yourself."

Eunice was delighted with the plan. There was no difficulty in thinking of any number of articles which were just what the children wanted; and Mrs. Ellett had a good excuse for asking questions now.

Aunt Dora was commissioned to do the shopping, and she did not ask Eunice's com-

pany, this time. Mrs. Ellott did not wish her
to know the cost of the materials which were
to be laid to her hand. The good lady had
means of her own, and nothing delighted her
more than such an opportunity as this of
employing her peculiar talents, and her money,
for the benefit of others.

"Now if we only knew just the sizes we want!"
cried Aunt Dora, when the purchases were
brought home, and spread upon Aunt Mildred's
bed.

But this difficulty was easily met: Rhoda
Merritt had two little sisters, just the age, and,
as Eunice felt sure, just the size of Bess and
Susy, and the dimensions of apron and frock
patterns were obtained from them.

Aunt Dora did the cutting and fitting; as
she declared nobody in that house had a right
to "flourish the shears" but herself!

Aunt Edith's machine lightened the work
considerably; and in various ways her kind
friends managed that Eunice should not be
overtasked in carrying out her scheme; while
yet the putting together, and finishing of each

article was done by herself. The girl's heart throbbed with grateful appreciation of all this kindness, which she valued far more than if the same amount of labor and expenditure had been bestowed upon herself.

"Eunice," said her uncle, one day, while the box was under consideration, "I must add some toys, and such like, as my contribution to that box; and I commission you to select them for me; you will know best how to please the young folks." And he placed a ten-dollar bill in her hand.

"Oh, Uncle Ransom! you are *so* kind!" cried Eunice. This was just what she was secretly wishing for; just a *few* playthings, to make the eyes of the little ones dance. "But this is too much for toys, isn't it?" she said; examining the bill with surprise.

"Oh, I will trust you to make very wise selections; consider it as your own spending money, daughter; and use it as you please; you will not find it any too much, I assure you!"

"But you needn't buy a doll for Bess; that is my special look out," said her Aunt Edith.

Three days before Christmas, in time to be sure that the box should reach its destination, by express, there was a grand packing in Aunt Mildred's room ;—it was done there because the invalid was not able to leave her room, being more poorly than usual ; and she was as much interested as Eunice in the business.

"It was as good as a medicine," Aunt Mildred declared, "to watch the happy face, beaming over the box."

There were some warm and pretty flannel shirts for George ; Eunice remembered that her mother had his old ones in her mending basket, when she came away, to be patched up, and the sleeves elongated, for another winter. There was a nice overcoat for Ranney ; and a warm bright comforter for each of the boys, which Aunt Mildred knit herself. Then there was the prettiest little dress, with sacque of the same, of soft plaid, for each of the dear little girls ; and some nice aprons, neatly made and trimmed, and some new warm flannel garments, for little Walter ; Eunice smiled as the doubt crossed her mind whether he had ever worn any new

flannel, so far, in his little life! The grandest
gift of all was a nice comfortable dressing-gown
for her father.

Eunice knew well how much her mother
wished to replace the old one, which had been
a great comfort to him, but was quite worn out.
She patted each fold, as she prepared to lay it
in the box, in a loving satisfied way, which fully
repaid Aunt Mildred for her part of the gift.

Surely the mother was not forgotten? No:
but Eunice had been more puzzled to decide
for her than for the others. She knew of
enough that was needed, but the articles being
all rather large, Eunice did not like to speak of
them, and Mrs. Ellett did not seem inclined to
urge her.

She would gladly have taken the best part of
the ten dollars for this gift; but that would
hardly be right, she thought, as her uncle
designed it for the children.

So, reflecting that her mother would enjoy
each of the other gifts more than if it were
for herself alone, Eunice was obliged to be
satisfied with making up a little box of 'medleys'

for her darling mother, two neat little collars, which she had made herself, lying on top. She had written a little note, bidding her mother fancy all the cracks and interstices crammed with love, when Aunt Edith came to the door with a parcel in her hand.

"I hope there is room for this, my dear? O yes; the box is not nearly full yet."

"But, auntie, what in the world is that?"

"Read and see, Miss Curiosity."

Eunice read, with a glowing face:

"For Mrs. Somers; from all the household at No 74; a token of gratitude for the loan of her 'right-hand man.'"

"Oh, Aunt Edith!" was all that Eunice could say.

"Would you like a peep?" said Aunt Edith, opening one end of the parcel.

"Oh, let her see it; spread it out!" said Aunt Mildred.

A cloak; actually a new cloak! how long since her mother had had one! And a dress pattern of some serviceable winter goods, besides!

"From all in the house? where shall I begin to give thanks?" said Eunice, merrily.

"One would suppose the parcel was for *you*, missie; but it is no such thing!" said Aunt Edith, folding the cloak again.

"But if you will undertake the thanks, you must begin with Dick; it was his suggestion that we should unite in a gift."

Eunice did not forget to 'begin,' as soon as her cousin came home.

Aunt Edith's skill was needed to finish packing the box.

The doll for Bess was a beauty; no such doll had been seen in the Somers' house since the days of Lucilla the Fair; indeed the charms of this new 'Heart's delight' even exceeded the memory of hers.

There was a grand new knife, and an interesting book for George; and various toys and other matters for- Ranney and the little ones; the selection of which had cost the sister much careful consideration, in deciding which playthings would last longest, and best serve the purpose of keeping the young ones amused,

and out of their mother's way. The choice
did credit to her experience as an elder sister;
though it is fair to say that she had the advice
of Rhoda Merritt in this important business.

At last the box was nailed up and directed;
and Eunice felt as if she could hardly wait for
the happy letter which should describe its
reception at home.

"How devoted the child is to her parents,
and brothers and sisters!" quoth Mrs. Ellett,
to her sister-in-law; "I think I never saw
a more loving daughter; she seems to have
noticed and treasured up every want and wish
of her mother's."

Mrs. Hartwell assented; smiling to herself as
she thought how much easier it was to remember the wants of friends, backed by a ready
purse, in filling a Christmas-box, than to
minister to these same dear ones, by self-
denial, in the daily needs of home-life. She
was, however, really pleased with the thoughtful love evinced by her niece in this matter,
and felt quite satisfied that her plan was
working well, in this respect, as in others.

One more preparation for Christmas, besides those already mentioned, had pleasantly occupied Eunice's time and thoughts; that was, making ready a little token of affection for each member of her uncle's family. She had been occasionally furnished with spending money, by the same indulgent uncle; and having but few wants, had been able to reserve most of it for this purpose.

Miss Lynde was a most kind and efficient helper in this matter; suggesting suitable articles, and showing her how to make them, during sundry pleasant afternoon visits proposed for that purpose, which made Aunt Edith wonder at the rapid growth of the intimacy between the two. Eunice did not forget to reserve from her little fund a special offering for Christmas day; she did not *quite* forget to whose Hand she owed all her present happiness.

Christmas has a right to one chapter of our " Winter's Tale:" but we should exceed that limit if a full description were given of the pleasures of the festive season. Enough to

6

say that the work of the happy hours of preparation just referred to, was accepted with pleased surprise ; and Eunice found, on the Christmas morning, that her friends had in turn well remembered her.

The Christmas Tree at St. James' was a most gratifying success, and the faithful band of parish workers felt amply rewarded for their exertions by the delightful Christmas services in which they participated, in their little church.

Many happy auguries passed from lip to lip, of an increase of prosperity to their infant parish, as a result of their Christmas tide

And the letter from Mansfield ? Aye, it was duly received ; and read by Eunice first, with both tears and smiles ; and then by each one in the house with sympathizing pleasure. For it spoke of the unbounded joy of the little ones over their treasures ; and of the uplifting of a load of care from the parents, by the well-timed gifts ; and it was full of the true spirit of Christmas ;—thankful, reverent joy.

CHAPTER VII.

A Cloud Arises.

"We need as much the cross we bear
As air we breathe,—as light we see;
It draws us to Thy side in prayer,
It binds us to our strength in Thee."

THE Christmas season was over; and Eunice, realizing that her precious winter was nearly half gone, applied herself with redoubled energy to her studies, and to her drawing. She seemed remarkably well, and her friends had quite given up their anxieties lest she should injure herself by application to study, as she declared she had never felt so strong, and so free from " aches and ails," since she could remember.

Miss Lynde, who was becoming more and more attached to her loving young friend and

(83)

pupil, was the means of imparting a cheerful
variety to her daily life, calling often for her
company in a walk, generally with some
special object of interest in view; and inviting
her frequently to her own house.

Dick North declared himself quite jealous of
this growing and strengthening friendship.
At which Eunice only smiled, for she had
reason to suspect that he visited Miss Frances
quite as often as she did, to say the least!

The girls, her classmates in Sunday-school,
proved very pleasant acquaintances. But
among them all, to her aunt's surprise, she
seemed to care most for the quiet Rhoda.

As has been before hinted, Eunice was at
first led to notice Rhoda by her evident liking
for herself; but, as she knew her better, she
became deeply interested in the shy, unassum-
ing girl; though she could hardly have explained why. Eunice was warmly welcomed
at the home of her young friend, and urged to
visit them often, which she was not reluctant to
do.

Like herself, Rhoda was the oldest of a

large family of children; and though there was
not the same need of her aid and efforts, in
one sense, as the Merritts were in easy circumstances, yet there were, as in every large
family, manifold claims upon the sympathy
and good offices of the elder sister. Eunice
felt herself fascinated in observing the conduct
of her friend Rhoda, in this respect.

The younger children seemed to think there
was no one like "sister" to help them out
of any difficulty; but however frequent and
impatient the calls upon her attention, Eunice
never heard from her a vexed or angry word.
She always met the little claimants with a
gentle smile, listened with patient interest to
their wants and woes, and if she were not able
to grant the request urged, she would at least
soothe them, and divert their attention to
something else.

"Rhoda, how can you be so patient? I
wonder at you!"

This exclamation was forced from the lips of
Eunice one day, when she was spending an
hour or two with her friend. She was trying

to show her a new "tatting" pattern which she had learned of Miss Lynde. Rhoda was quite eager to learn it; but in the midst of her occupation she was interrupted three or four times, by the children; one begging to know if she could find his ball; another toddling up with the request, "Pease make my dolly's dress stay on!" and so on.

Rhoda laughed at Eunice's remark, and answered merrily: "It is my best policy, you see; I can satisfy them a great deal sooner if I keep quiet, myself! And besides," she added, a little gravely, "I never can forget a little verse my mother taught me when I was about as old as Florie, there:

> " Be kind to each other,
>   The time's coming on
> When sister or brother
>   Perhaps may be gone !"

Eunice was perplexed by the peculiar tone with which Rhoda repeated these simple lines; she seemed to have a meaning beyond her words; and as Eunice looked questioningly in her face, she was about to say more; but her mother entered the room at that moment, and she playfully changed the subject.

The matter recurred more than once to Eunice's mind, after she returned home. "Can Rhoda be ill in any way, so bright and lively as she seems?" thought she. Then she suddenly recollected how, more than once, when she had been with Rhoda, a pallid look had overspread her face, when she was slightly startled or excited; and sometimes she had seen her press her hand upon her side; but when Eunice asked if anything was the matter, she had received an evasive reply.

Eunice felt uneasy about her friend, and asked her aunt if she knew of her being out of health. But Mrs. Hartwell did not, and seemed surprised at the question: "She has the appearance of perfect health, I think," she observed.

Eunice intended to question Rhoda the next time they met; but she saw her again, in a day or two, at Miss Lynde's, and Rhoda seemed so happy and lively, with her two favorite friends, that Eunice smiled at the remembrance of her anxieties.

February had come; and Eunice, reminding herself of the fact, as she dressed herself, on the first morning of the short month, felt almost sorry that she had allowed herself to be beguiled into visiting, or spending any time in amusement.

"I *must* prepare longer lessons for uncle;" she murmured to herself; "he will attend to me as long as I can recite; and I must get on faster! And my drawing! Positively that piece must be finished to-day!"

One or two interruptions during her study hours, only increased the girl's desire to finish her self-imposed task.

Dinner was delayed that evening, and Eunice worked on at her drawing until the bell rang; although, it being a dull, cloudy day, the light was unusually dim, even for that twilight hour.

"Come, little daughter! Are you here?" called her uncle, opening the library door, on his way to the dining-room. "What! not *drawing*, at ever so much past. five o'clock! You are very imprudent, my dear child; you should take better care of your precious eye-sight!"

As her uncle spoke, Eunice felt painfully conscious of the justice of his remonstrance. She had been annoyed, more than once, within a few days past, by a slight sensation of pain and weakness of the eyes. Never having experienced any difficulty of the kind before, she had paid no attention to it; but this hour's work, with very insufficient light, had greatly aggravated the troublesome symptoms. Eunice determined secretly not to read or draw at twilight again; and not to touch a book that evening, except during her recitation hour.

She was heartily glad to find that her cousin Dick was to be at home that evening, and to hear him propose a game of backgammon. The said game was quite tiresome to Eunice, generally; and she only took part in it out of politeness to Dick, or to gratify Aunt Mildred, who was very fond of it.

Eunice bathed her eyes carefully when she retired that night; but with all her care, the next morning they were much inflamed, and

pained her a good deal. Happily, as she
fancied, no one observed their condition, when
the family assembled for prayers and breakfast.
Eunice smuggled a small bowl of water into
the library with her, to bathe her eyes frequently, hoping thus to be able to pursue her
studies.

"I *must* study!" she ejaculated; "eyes or no
eyes."

It was well for the reckless girl that Aunt
Dora peeped into the library in the course of
an hour:

"Eunice, my love, I am afraid it is too cold
here for you: the furnace fire appears to
be bewitched this morning; it will not throw
out any heat! Come into the sitting-room
with us awhile; we will not disturb you."

As Eunice glanced up to reply, Miss Dora
exclaimed, in alarm:

"Why, my *dear* child! what ails your eyes?
They seem to be fearfully inflamed. Do they
not pain you? And here you are using them
in this condition! Put away these books, this
instant!"

And without awaiting the answer to her queries, the little woman bustled out of the room, as Eunice knew, to give the alarm. Sure enough, in a few moments she was summoned to an anxious consultation.

Mrs. Hartwell was really worried, on examining the poor eyes, and finding from Eunice's reluctant answers, how long the trouble had been coming on. One prescribed one thing, and another something quite different, until, as Eunice thought to herself, with an inward laugh, " her eyes were in peril of being washed out."

But all agreed upon a few points; namely, that Eunice must not use her eyes in the least; and must wear a shade, and avoid a bright light.

Poor child! This was no laughing matter. But her friends exerted themselves to while away the tedious hours, and she could not but feel grateful for their sympathy. And besides, she might only lose one day, or perhaps two; by taking care of her eyes, surely they would soon be well!

But the trouble was too deeply seated to be so easily overcome. The pain in her eyes rather increased than diminished towards evening; and when Mr. Hartwell came home to dinner, and heard his wife's report, and examined the eyes, he at once declared that it was not a matter to be trifled with.

"Dr. Williams is considerable of an oculist;" said he; "I suppose he could hardly pronounce upon the case at night, but I will get him to call early to-morrow morning."

"In the mean time, my dear, be very careful, and do not use your eyes at all."

Poor Eunice suffered too much with the offending members to be in any danger of disregarding this command.

Her uncle very kindly proposed reading aloud, and chose an entertaining book for the evening; but Eunice felt too uneasy in body and mind to enjoy it very much. The thought *would* present itself, again and again: "What if my eyes should grow worse, and I should have to give up my drawing, and all my studies!"

At an early hour she crept away to bed, and

cried herself to sleep : which did not improve the state of the poor eyes.

Dr. Williams called the next morning, and made a careful examination. He was a man of few words, and was proceeding to make out a prescription, when Eunice exclaimed :

"Doctor, please say that I may study very soon again ; it will not hurt me to use my eyes carefully, will it ?"

"My dear young lady, you are not to think of studying at present ; I fear it will require many days of rest and careful nursing to make your eyes well and strong again."

The words smote like lead upon Eunice's heart.

When the doctor had given Mrs. Hartwell his directions, and left the house, Eunice went up to her own room. Not now to weep ; she felt too gloomy for that relief ; a sullen feeling, almost of despair, held possession of her soul.

After waiting some time for her to come down, Mrs. Hartwell went up to her room, and found Eunice still lying on the bed, with her face hidden in the pillows.

"Come, my child," said her aunt, cheerily, "do not feel so badly. I am going round to the apothecary's to have this lotion prepared, and I want you to go with me. I will lend you my thick green veil, and it is so mild and pleasant this morning it will do you good to walk out a little.

"Then we must stop and let Mr. Neville know why you cannot be with the class to-day. Cheer up, and we will hope you will soon be well again. When we come back from our walk we will see what else we can find to do, to pass away the time."

All in the house were full of sympathy for Eunice in her trial, and ready to do all in their power to alleviate it; but they did not succeed in recalling the cheerful smile and happy look which they had loved to see.

The heart of the young girl was full of bitter, rebellious thoughts.

"Mother said well that I could not escape the cross," she murmured, in the solitude of her own room, where she would gladly have stayed all the day; "but oh! if it might have been anything but this. To have to give up all that I came here for, and lose all my opportunities :—it is *too* hard !"

Mrs. Hartwell wrote to her sister, informing her of Eunice's trouble.

"The doctor told us, privately," she wrote, "that he feared it was a case which would require long and patient treatment. In fact, though I hope his remedies may sooner effect a cure, it is quite possible that the poor child may not be able to use her eyes much this spring.

"I anticipate your probable reply to this, my dear sister; and hasten to beg that you will not urge her return home just yet.

"At present she is so much depressed by the disappointment, and the sudden interruption of her pursuits, that we cannot seem to say much to comfort her. But we hope, in a day or two, she will become more reconciled to her trial; and we are planning various ways to carry on a course of instruction, without the eyes.

"There is to be a series of scientific lectures,

during the next three or four weeks, to which cousin Dick proposes to take her.

"Then, either sister Mildred, Dora, or I can read to her aloud, in history, and other useful works; fixing the lesson by questions.

"The interruption to her drawing, in which she was making very rapid progress, is the most trying part of all; but then there is the hope that she may soon be able to resume it; if she were to give up this hope, as she would in returning home now, it would be very hard for her."

Mrs. Somers' reply was addressed to Eunice:

MANSFIELD, *Feb.* 8.

"MY DARLING DAUGHTER:

"Your Aunt Edith's letter is received, and I feel that I must write at once, to-night, to tell you how much we feel for you, in your trouble.

"Your father and I know well that this is a severe trial to our eager, ambitious Eunie; and we hope and pray that our dear girl has sought of the Lord grace to bear this trial submissively and cheerfully, as a Christian should.

" Perhaps, my love, there was need that you should pause awhile in a prosperous and joyous career, and look within. Perhaps our Lord saw that amid the abundance of His good gifts there was danger that you might forget the Giver.

"Try to feel assured, my Eunice, that all which He orders is for the best.

> " 'Whate'er my God ordains is right ;
> My Light, my Life is He,
> Who cannot will me aught but good,
> I trust Him utterly:
> For well I know,
> In joy or woe,
> We soon shall see, as sunlight clear,
> How faithful was our Guardian here.'

" Your kind auntie seems to be devising ways to keep you pleasantly occupied still : say to her, with my love, that I think she is right, and that I thank her heartily for all her kindness.

"Good-by, my dear child ; I trust your dark hours will be brightened by faith, hope, and love.   MOTHER."

Eunice silently handed this letter to her Aunt

7

Edith to read, in reply to her questioning look; and, when it was returned, retreated with it to her own room.

She knew she must not pore over it, with her bodily eyes; but there was no need; the words of the letter had served to arouse a train of thought;—self-accusing, reproachful thoughts, they were.

"How ungrateful they must have thought me here!" she whispered, "to be so sullen, when they are all doing so much to comfort me."

And conscience added: "How ungrateful I have been to my Heavenly Father! 'Shall we receive good at the hand of the Lord, and shall we not receive evil?'"

These salutary musings were interrupted by a summons to the parlor, where Eunice found her friend Miss Lynde.

She had heard of the young girl's trouble, and called at once to sympathize with, and cheer her.

She proposed to go over the lesson for the next day with Eunice, it being Saturday, that she might be prepared with the class.

The next day was Septuagesima Sunday; and Eunice's reflections upon her mother's letter had so humbled her that she was able sincerely to make the words of the Collect her own :

"We beseech Thee favorably to hear the prayers of Thy people; that we who are justly punished for our offences, may be mercifully delivered by Thy goodness, for the glory of Thy name."

CHAPTER VIII.

The Clouds Show the Silver Lining.

"Thy truer self to thee returns,
  A higher hope within thee glows.
. . . .
"Nothing too costly to lay down
  For Him whose smile pays every loss:
  Could we but see it, there's a crown
  Hangs, halo like, round every cross."

UNDAY over, Eunice showed the benefit of its means of grace, by entering with a comparatively cheerful and hopeful spirit, upon the new arrangements proposed for her. Her eyes were no better, that she could perceive, except that she suffered less actual pain than when the acute attack first came on. She was very faithful in applying the prescribed remedies; and Dr. Williams encouraged her by saying that she was doing better than he had at first anticipated: Eunice

(100)

mentally wondered what he could have anticipated worse than this!

The doctor was of opinion that with due
caution in protecting the eyes from the light,
and from dust and wind, his young patient
would do better with as much out-door exercise as she had been accustomed to ; perhaps
even more. It was desirable, he told her aunt,
to keep up the tone of her general health, and
her cheerfulness of mind.

So there was no objection to the attendance
upon the scientific lectures, guarding carefully
against a chill in coming out into the night
air.

At least, so Mrs. Hartwell thought; but, the
day after attending the second lecture, the poor
eyes were so much worse, that it was evident it
would not do for Eunice to go out at night.

This was a new disappointment, for Eunice
had already become very much interested in
the course ; but she was learning her lesson of
patient submission, and bore this decision very
cheerfully. .

Her cousin Dick was quite impressed by her

manner, knowing well how much she had enjoyed the lectures.

"I believe," said he, "it was watching the experiments, that tried her eyes, more than being out in the evening. There is to be a pretty good concert next week, Tuesday; can I take her to that? She can listen to the music with her eyes shut."

It was well that Eunice was out of hearing of this tempting proposal; she was nearly as fond of music as of drawing, and had thoroughly enjoyed the two or three concerts to which she had been treated, during the winter.

Mrs. Hartwell shook her head: "The hall will be brightly lighted," she said, "and I am afraid there will be a good deal of risk: it is better to be on the safe side."

History flourished, almost as well as if the young student had the use of her eyes. Mrs. Hartwell read remarkably well, so that it was a pleasure to listen to her: she asked questions, at the close of each reading, reviewing occasionally.

For another exercise, she read choice

passages of prose or poetry, which Ennice was to analyze and parse.

Mr. Hartwell declared he would not be deprived of his hour with his pupil, after dinner; and with a good deal of ingenuity, he managed that she should not lose, but really make additional progress in her Latin; exercising her in a review of the Grammar, and in translating passages which he read to her.

He also carried on a very improving mental drill in mathematics; and laughingly declared that if other professions failed, he should set himself up as a teacher of the blind.

Mrs. Ellett continued quite feeble; indeed, had Eunice not been disabled, she would hardly have been able to continue the sewing lessons.

During the rebellious days after the trouble with her eyes began, Eunice scarcely saw her gentle old friend. Mrs. Ellett was not able to go down to meals, or to enjoy her customary drives; and Eunice avoided her room, because she could not bear to be questioned about her eyes.

On the afternoon of that Sunday on which a better spirit took possession of her heart, she went in to sit with the old lady awhile after church, and was so warmly and affectionately greeted that her heart smote her for her negligence.

"I thought my darling had forgotten that Aunt Mildred was here, wishing for her sunbeam."

"I am afraid I have not been a sunbeam to any one, lately," returned Eunice, kissing the soft hand she held.

"It does me good to see a bright young face, my dear; and yours cannot be overcast long, because you know who chooses for us our good and ill."

And little Aunt Dora, how was her sympathy manifested? Firstly, in her own most natural way; by keeping watch over Eunice's wardrobe, with additional care, "because the poor child couldn't take a stitch for herself, now." To say truth, never had her mending been so neatly and thoroughly done, since it fell into the young lady's charge, as now.

One morning, Miss Dora had come into Eunice's room with some stockings which she had darned, as Eunice was dusting her bureau. A half sigh escaped her, as she placed in an orderly pile her Bible and Prayer-book, and one or two little books for private devotional reading. Meeting Miss Dora's glance, she said : " It seems so strange that I must not use these !"

" Have you a 'Daily Food,' my dear? I mean a little book with a text for each day, you know."

Eunice had not : and Miss Dora left the room, returning in a moment with a tiny volume in her hand.

" I will give you this, my dear, if you will accept it; and I must tell you why I thought of it.

" I had a friend once who for many years had been unable to walk, except a few steps with crutches. She lay on her back through the greater part of every day. And this was not all; she was afflicted also with some disease of the eyes, so that she could not use them at all, in reading or sewing.

"But she always kept a copy of this little Daily Food under her pillow. 'Her eyes *must* serve her,' she said, 'to read one verse a day for herself;' though for all beside she must depend upon the kind offices of others. So I thought, my dear, you might like to adopt the same plan."

Eunice thankfully received the little volume, saying it was just what she wanted.

Miss Dora smoothed the bureau cover with her fingers, hesitatingly, and then added : "If you would like it, my dear,—seeing that you cannot read for yourself,—you might come to my room between nine and ten in the morning ; that is, when I get through my little chores about the house, you know.

"I have a quiet little time to myself then ; and if you have a mind to come in, I can read aloud, and so share my portion with you ; we will each try to feel as if we were all alone."

"I should like to, Aunt Dora; thank you; is it time now?" said Eunice.

Miss Dora assented, and led the way to her own room; a small chamber which was exclusively hers, although she generally slept with her invalid charge.

Eunice would have been sorry to betray how much she was surprised by this proposal. Miss Dora was the last one of the household, Dick excepted, from whom she would have expected it. She had formed her own opinion of the bustling little woman, as one whose religion was rather overgrown by worldliness. How ashamed she felt of her self-satisfied comparisons, and uncharitable judgments, while seated by her Aunt Dora's side, that morning!

The offer had not been made without a struggle on the part of the humble-minded Christian, who was not accustomed to vaunt her piety; and it was with a somewhat tremulous tone that she began her customary reading, in the presence of another. Gradually the tremor disappeared, and the reader seemed absorbed in her occupation, as if unconscious of an auditor, or only remembering that she too needed the "water" which she was seeking to draw, "from the wells of salvation."

These third-hour devotions consisted in

reading the psalms for the day, and the second morning lesson ; also a few passages from " The Imitation of Christ," or some other work of similar character, and a brief arrangement of prayers for the hour, which called forth the soul of the youthful Christian, in unison with their fervent words, as they were meekly uttered by her companion. When they arose from their knees, Eunice gave this true friend a kiss, and a whispered " Thank you," and quietly left the room.

To no one else did she speak of this privilege, as she felt it to be ; but it proved a great help to her during the season of trial which had but just begun.

Frances Lynde was by no means forgetful of the added claims of her young friend upon her attention.

Eunice greatly enjoyed running around to spend an hour or two with her, and was fully satisfied to sit beside her, watching her at work, and listening to her pleasant and improving talk ; and more than satisfied if Miss Lynde remembered to lay down the work awhile and play for her, or sing, with her rich voice, some touching ballad, or sacred melody.

"Do you never sing yourself, Eunice?" she asked once, impressed with her evident enjoyment of the music.

"I? O no! At least, I used to at home, after my fashion; just to put baby to sleep."

Miss Lynde smiled, and was about to ask her to sing a familiar strain with her, to test her voice; but was interrupted by some callers. A day or two afterward, she called at Mrs. Hartwell's in the morning, and finding Eunice with her aunt, said playfully:

"I am come to take this benighted girl, with your permission, to hear a rehearsal of the oratorio which is to be performed to-morrow evening; I think this is the last rehearsal, and it will be about as fine as the actual performance."

"I shall be delighted to have her hear it," said Mrs. Hartwell; "it is very kind of you to think of her. Run, my dear, and get ready; we will excuse the history to-day."

Eunice was not long in dressing, and soon

re-appeared, with eyes that danced in spite of their ailing.

"Let me tie your veil closely, dear; there is a good deal of wind this morning. Mrs. Hart-well, do not be surprised if you do not see this troublesome charge of yours until nightfall. I suppose I must not keep her out for the evening, but I want her all day."

It was the Oratorio of The Messiah, to which Eunice was privileged to listen that morning; it was really well performed; and no lover of good music need be told how she enjoyed it. ·

The Lyndes dined at two, so that they were summoned to dinner soon after they reached the house.

Perhaps the excitement of the morning and the absence of luncheon, had something to do with it, but Eunice fancied it was the earlier hour which gave her such an excellent appetite; she had never become quite used to the late dinners which her uncle's business made neces-sary.

After dinner Miss Lynde was obliged to leave her young guest by herself for a short time;

and, returning unexpectedly to the parlor, she was surprised to hear her singing to herself one of the airs from the oratorio they had just heard.

She played the part of listener for a few moments, until the young singer became conscious that she was likely to be heard, and ceased suddenly.

Then she entered, and said, merrily, "What voice could I have overheard, warbling that aria? There is no one here but a child, who says she cannot sing."

Eunice blushed ; but her friend went on :

"Seriously, my dear child, I judge from that little performance that you have quite a sweet voice, as well as a quick ear for music ; come, let us try it again, together."

Miss Lynde had the music of the aria, which was "Come unto Me ;" and having found it, and placed it open upon the piano, she called Eunice to her side, and insisted that she should try it with her.

Eunice's voice was weak and frightened at first ; but on going over the piece the second time, she gained confidence, and came out upon the high notes with a sweet, clear tone which delighted her friend.

"My dear, I am afraid one of your talents has been quite undervalued and lost sight of; but I am determined it shall be so no longer."

"Do you know," continued Miss Lynde, in her sprightly way, wheeling round upon the piano stool, and seizing Eunice's hands in her own, I am very selfishly glad to have made this discovery just now."

"*Why*, pray?"

"Because, you remember, Lent begins next week; Mr. Robertson likes to have at least a hymn at the early services, if we cannot have the chants; but it is very hard getting our singers to attend, and so, as I do not like to disappoint him, or to have the service entirely without music, I have often been obliged to lead off all alone. But now I shall rely upon having a helper always on hand.

"And we will make a bargain, if your aunt is willing. You shall help me in the choir; and I will give you lessons;—that is, you know, we

EUNICE AND MISS LYNDE.—PAGE 112.

will have little private rehearsals of our own; and I will teach you all I can without calling the eyes into request too much."

There was no need to ask if this plan was satisfactory; at least the latter part of it. Eunice had never had any instruction in music. She shrank a little from the idea of singing in church, but would not refuse, if she could really help Miss Lynde in her somewhat arduous duties.

And so a new and unexpected opportunity for usefulness, and self-improvement, opened up before Eunice; for her Aunt Edith, far from objecting, was much gratified by Miss Lynde's kind proposition; though surprised by her opinion of her niece's voice and musical taste, having seldom heard her attempt to sing.

8

CHAPTER IX.

Rhoda.

"Teach us, as we pass along,
    In the shining of Thy face.
Many a sweet thanksgiving song,
    Even in a *dreary* place. . . . . . .

"In the shadow of Thy hand
    We can brave the uprooting gale;
And a little child may stand
    Where a soldier's heart would fail."

 LETTER from her mother informed Eunice that Ranney had had a fall, the effects of which alarmed them for a time; but that he seemed to be getting over it nicely, and they had relinquished their fears of permanent injury.

The same letter stated that Mr. Somers was gaining constantly, and was better able to attend to business than he had been in two or three years. "The children are well; and

(114)

we are all getting on finely," continued the writer.

" The children were preparing their Sunday-school lessons together, last week : Ranney received the explanation that the word *Lent* means 'Spring.'

" Bessie overheard it, and exclaimed, joyfully, ' Oh ! Then if spring is most here, it will soon be time for Eunice to come home, for she was to stay " all winter," and winter is done !'

" You see, darling, that your return is joy-fully looked forward to by those at home.

" Aunt Edith and Bessie would disagree in the application of the term ' all winter ;' but I suppose we may look for you at home soon after Easter, although I shall defer to your auntie's wishes in setting a time for your return. In the mean time, be assured that we all love you dearly, and shall be glad to see you when the time comes."

Eunice was preparing to go and see Rhoda, when this letter was received, and it gave her food for thought, as she walked along.

" To-morrow is Ash Wednesday ; yes, and it

is the very last day of winter, at least of the winter months. How soon Easter will be here! And I cannot begin to use my eyes yet: my drawing lessons are over, I am afraid;—oh dear!"

Just then, in turning a corner, she encountered Mr. Neville.

"Ah, Miss Somers, well met! I have been wishing to be able to call and inquire after my truant pupil. The eyes are well, by this time, I hope; you have not lost your interest in our beautiful art, have you?"

"No, indeed!" Eunice protested; and explained that she was not yet permitted the use of her eyes.

Mr. Neville looked a little incredulous, and expressing the hope that she might soon recover, bowed and passed on.

"I wonder if the man thinks I don't *care* to pursue my lessons?" muttered Eunice, quite vexed.

On the whole, she was not in the most amiable of moods when she reached the house of her friend.

Rhoda soon perceived the lack of her usual cheerful manner, and after a one-sided chat, prolonged for some little time, ventured to inquire what had disturbed her friend.

"Oh, nothing new!" replied Eunice; "only I met Mr. Neville on the way, and was reminded afresh of my disappointment."

"About your eyes? Mr. Neville was your drawing-teacher, I believe?"

"Yes: oh, Rhoda! you can't begin to understand how hard it is! I thought I was getting on so well; and I was trying so hard to improve this precious winter! *Why* should I be laid aside in this way? I cannot feel as if it were right!"

"Oh, Eunice dear! You do not mean that! You and I know better."

"Ah! It is very easy to 'know,' and to 'talk;' but if you had such a trial, you would not find it easy always to *feel* just right."

"No; it is not always easy, but we can get help, you know, dear."

"Wait until *you* are put out in all your plans, and see if you don't feel naughty some-

times. You have nothing in the world to try
you yet, and you cannot understand."

"Oh, Eunice!" The exclamation was almost
a cry, as if the words of her friend hurt her;
but Rhoda added instantly, in her own quiet
tone: "I think I can understand, dear; perhaps
I have a trial too, though I do not want to feel
it such."

Eunice glanced wonderingly at the speaker,
and again she noticed the sudden paleness
which she had observed before.

"Rhoda, what do you mean? Please tell
me. Are you ill?" she asked, passing her
arm affectionately around her companion's
waist.

Rhoda paused before answering, and Eunice
perceived that this pause, so habitual with her,
and which had the appearance of hesitation
and shyness, was in order to gain calmness;
for she could feel the rapid beating of her
heart, and was surprised at her seeming agita-
tion.

"I thought you knew, Eunice,—at least, my
friends generally know, that I have a disease of

the heart, which may at any time cause my death."

Eunice with difficulty repressed the startled exclamation which rose to her lips. She did not trust herself to speak, but clasped Rhoda's hand with a loving pressure which spoke her sympathy.

"I used to think, before I knew this," continued Rhoda, "that I should *so* love to study,—to study real hard, I mean, as you like to do. But you see, all I can do now, is to try to keep quiet, and live a little longer for my dear parents' sake; *they* would miss their useless little girl."

This was said in a cheerful, even playful tone, and with a smile which went to the heart of her friend.

"Oh, Rhoda! And you are so patient and happy, with *this* before your mind; and I have been so rebellious, just because I have to stop for a little while. But I don't see how you can be so calm—so satisfied!" said Eunice, turning so as to look full in Rhoda's face.

All was explained now; that which had

so puzzled her, and that which had attracted her so much, in Rhoda.

Eunice recalled at once her manner with the little ones, and her reply, on that subject. She remembered, also, the peculiar watchful tenderness of her parents towards her, and also of Miss Lynde, and of some of her young companions : *they* had known, evidently; it was strange that Eunice had not learned this before.

"There! you have said it in the very words of my favorite hymn; the next line answers you,—the only answer I can give :

"So safe, so calm, so *satisfied*
  The souls that cling to Thee!

" Blest is our lot, whate'er befall :
  What can affright, or who appall?
  Since as our Strength, our Rock, our all,
  Jesus, we cling to Thee!"

" Dear Rhoda! Teach me to be like you. I wish I had your faith!"

"We are in the same school, Eunice, and we have the same ever kind teacher. *I* cannot teach you, but we will help each other learn; *wont we*?"

A smile, dimmed with tears, was all the answer Eunice could give.

"Aren't you glad that Lent begins to-morrow?" said Rhoda; "and we are to have daily services, at eight o'clock, you know; I do hope I shall be able to go to every one."

"I want to, too;" said Eunice, but I suppose I shall miss some; Aunt Edith is so particular about my going out when it is at all wet, on account of my eyes; and we are apt to have some damp mornings at this season."

"Mother says 'no' to me, sometimes, too; I have not felt quite as well as usual lately, and they are very careful of me. But we will go when we can, both of us, wont we?"

Eunice assented, and told Rhoda of her singing engagements with Miss Lynde.

"How nice! I am so glad for you. What a dear friend she is, isn't she?"

Another hearty assent. "How beautifully she explained, last Sunday," continued Eunice, "about the use of Lent; and how earnestly she talked to us."

"Yes: you know, Eunice, that you and I are the only ones in the class who are confirmed, and communicants; and Miss Lynde is very anxious to have Celia and Kitty, and the rest, prepared to come forward to the Confirmation, just after Easter."

"Perhaps *we* can help influence them; let us watch and see."

"Yes, we will," replied Rhoda, "but, do you know, I think you can do more in influencing them than I can; for when I say anything, they give me a pitying sort of look, as much as to say: 'No wonder you think of such things, with one foot in the grave, as it were.'"

"But you are strong and well as any of them! O Rhoda!" Eunice could not repress a shudder; "how can you speak so? It *does* seem as if it could not be as you think; how should the doctors know?"

"They don't know;—they cannot tell how long I may live;—it may be years—it may be but a few hours.

"Why should you feel so badly to hear me speak of it, dear? I am not afraid; my Father knows the time,—the *best* time.

"And after all, which of us can tell how soon we may be called to die? We all need to be ready, just the same."

Here little Florie ran in, claiming her sister's attention, which claim was never disregarded.

Eunice sat by, watching the movements of her friend, as in a dream.

"Poor Jack in the box! Does he want to come out and get some fresh air?

"But he is not hopelessly imprisoned," continued Rhoda, playfully. "Take care, pet; he will spring out and bump your little nose. There!"

And the bent catch being unfastened, up flew the cover, to the child's great delight.

Rhoda's eyes reflected the light-hearted glee of little Florie, as she turned again to Eunice.

Others of the family soon came in, and the talk became general. Indeed, it was not often that Rhoda spoke so much and so freely of her own feelings, as she had done that afternoon.

Eunice went home with a full heart, and could not soon put from her thoughts this conversation with her young friend.

In the evening, chancing to be alone, as she supposed, with Miss Dora, she began to tell her about Rhoda's situation.

It was easier now to speak to her, on any subject upon which she felt deeply, than to any one else in the house.

She was describing the calmness of her young friend, in speaking of her constant danger, when Dick emerged from a corner, where he had been half asleep in an easy chair, and joined in the conversation.

"Is it that quiet little Rhoda Merritt who is such a heroine?" he asked.

Eunice hesitated; she was sorry to find that he had overheard her, feeling that he would not understand.

"I do not think that word belongs to Rhoda," she said, at last; "not in the sense you mean, Cousin Dick."

"How then would *you* describe her?"

Eunice glanced at her Aunt Dora, hoping

she would come to the rescue; but her head was bent over her work.

"I think she is a real Christian;" she replied, in a low voice; and that is why she is not afraid to die."

Dick said nothing, but seemed waiting for Eunice to go on.

"But it is not only that she seems willing to *die* when the time comes: she is willing to *live,* just as she *must,* you know. I think that is the hardest thing, after all."

"*How* must she live?"

"Why, I mean, that she cannot follow out her plans;—she has to give up so many things, because she must not tire herself, or get excited. But she is so gentle and sweet; and so patient with the children. I think it is lovely!"

"And that, you would say, is an example of Christian faith?" said Dick.

There was no levity in his tone; and Eunice, meeting his glance, as she answered "Yes," was thrilled with a new pleasure.

"Did Cousin Dick understand? Did he really care?"

And while she rejoiced that he could appreciate the character of her young friend, Eunice felt humbled to think how little of the fruits of faith he had witnessed, in his daily intercourse with herself.

CHAPTER X.

Lenten Lessons.

"Think that He thy ways beholdeth:
He unfoldeth
Every fault that lurks within;
He the hidden shame glossed over
Can discover,
And discern each deed of sin."

N the services of Ash Wednesday, Eunice sang for the first time, beside her friend, in the choir.

It was a new experience to her, and the novelty might have drawn off her thoughts, in a great degree, from the solemn service, but for the example of reverent attention and devotion, which she had in Miss Lynde.

It was easy for her to follow the chants and tunes, which were simple and familiar; and Miss Lynde thanked her, after church, saying: "I know you will help me very much; and our

(127)

church is small; I do not think it will strain
your voice to sing in it. Did you not find it
easy?"

"O yes! I am sure it will do me no harm."

"We must try to feel what a privilege it is to
help thus in the worship of God's house," said
Miss Lynde, affectionately, drawing the hand of
her companion within her arm, as they turned
towards home: "and we must try to 'sing with
the spirit, and with the understanding also,' and
not render a heartless or unmeaning service."

"What a privilege it is!" This was, to say
the truth, a new thought to Eunice; she had
felt just a little lifted up at the idea of helping
the choir, as if she were doing something worthy
of thanks and praise.

Was she alone and singular in this respect?
Is it not too generally the feeling of those whom
God has gifted with 'tuneful powers,' that they
confer a favor upon Him, or at least, upon His
worshipping assembly, by employing this talent
in the service of His courts?

"Aunt Dora," whispered Eunice, that evening,
"what will you do now about our quiet hour?"

The daily service at church being appointed at eight, would interfere with the usual reading in Miss Dora's room.

"Of course, dear, we will give way to the public worship, and attend that, when we can. And we will try to secure a few moments at the 'ninth hour,'—that is about three o'clock, for our reading, if you like."

Thus Eunice began her Lent, fully purposing to make a diligent use of all her privileges and means of grace, and to abstain from everything which might hinder her in fulfilling this purpose.

Was she tempted to self-complacence in view of her resolves and arrangements? If so, before many days, she had a lesson upon her own weakness.

She had met one of her classmates, Celia Arnott, at the church door, after service one morning, and walked with her on her way to school.

The opportunity offered for a few serious words,—using her Christian influence, as Rhoda had urged her to do; and Eunice had not shrunk from the duty.

9

Returning home, with a secret self-satisfaction at her heart, she laid aside her things, and sought the rest of the family.

Mrs. Hartwell and Miss Dora, as she recollected, had gone on some errands after church. Mrs. Ellett's door was locked, and her gentle voice responded to Eunice's knock: "In a few moments, my love: I am sorry I am not quite ready!"

So Eunice strolled down-stairs: the library door was open, and she went in, and looked around.

"Dear books! Dear old chair! I wish I could sit right down and go to work! Ah! There is the book uncle was speaking of, as so interesting!"

Eunice peeped within the covers; a sentence attracted her, and she read it, and then another, and a page beyond; and so on, forgetful of all else, until brought to herself by a sudden darting pain through her eyes.

At the same moment, she heard her Aunt Edith's voice, as she opened the hall door; and, conscious how long she must have been reading, she sped up-stairs to her own room, like a guilty thing.

"How could I? oh, how *could* I do it!" she exclaimed, penitently bathing the ill-used eyes. "When I cannot even read my Bible, and ought to try so hard to get well!"

Very humbling were her reflections, as she dwelt upon her fault, while awaiting her Aunt Edith's summons to her history lesson; but perhaps they were more profitable, and more in accordance with the spirit of the season, than the feelings of some previous hours.

This was Friday. The next morning, after service, Eunice went home with Miss Lynde, for her music lesson, as she styled it, and as in truth it was; although the appellation excited the teacher's merriment.

"Pray do not describe my method of teaching, my dear," she said, "if you undertake to recommend me as a music teacher;—or at least explain that my pupil was forbidden to use her eyes! By the way, how are those eyes? I have been hoping to hear you say that they were ever so much better!"

" They are not better *to-day*," replied Eunice, blushing ; —"and it is all through my fault," she continued, moved to confess her wrong-doing to this kind and true friend.

"That is a specimen of *my* self-denial ; — losing all that my eyes had gained, in reading a romance ;—and one, too, that uncle had promised to read aloud to us, some time !

"Oh, Miss Lynde ! the harder I try to be good, the worse I grow ! "

"Not so, my darling ! But the more sincerely you try to be good, the more plainly you see that you 'have no power to help yourself,' as our collect for to-morrow expresses it :—have you studied that collect yet ? "

Eunice had not ; and her friend brought the book, proposing that they should go over the lesson together.

" Please read it again : what a precious collect that is ! " said Eunice, earnestly.

"Almighty God, who seest that we have no power of ourselves to help ourselves, keep us both outwardly in our bodies, and inwardly in our souls ; that we may be defended from all adversities which may happen to the body, and from all evil thoughts which may assault and hurt the soul; through Jesus Christ our Lord."

"Yes; it is a precious collect!" said Miss Lynde; "it is just what my dear girl wants, in every way; is it not?" she added, putting her hand, meaningly, upon her companion's eyes.

"I do not deserve to have the prayer answered in *that* way!" said Eunice.

"No, dear; and we do not ask for our *deserts*, but for mercies through Christ our Lord, and in submission to His will!

"I think there is no collect which I love more than this;" continued Miss Lynde, mus-ingly;—"it always reminds me of a dear friend, to whom it was very precious.

"She lay, helpless and suffering, upon her death-bed; and when this Second Sunday in Lent came, she asked, as usual, to have its special portion read to her.

"Repeating the words of this collect, she exclaimed with a bright and happy smile: 'Oh! is not that just what I want? Those words are meant for me, now!'"

"Oh, Miss Lynde!" cried Eunice, do you know about Rhoda Merritt? I mean what the physicians think about her? Isn't it terrible!"

"It does not seem to be, to *her*, my dear; she is able to trust herself in the Lord's hands."

"Oh, yes! And, Miss Lynde, seeing her act and feel as she does, makes me feel sure,— more so than I ever did before,—about the things we believe!"

"I have no doubt it does, dear; we can none of us tell how much good has been done by the example of her simple, earnest faith and piety."

Eunice thought of Dick's interest in her account of Rhoda, and was about to speak of it; but checked herself.

She had fancied there was more than a cousinly esteem and interest in this case, and shrank from mentioning what might have been but the impression of the moment, lest she should awaken hopes without foundation.

The pleasant and profitable morning having passed, Eunice was on the point of returning home, when the door-bell sounded, and Mr. Robertson entered.

He greeted his young parishioners warmly, but refused a seat; saying that he had just stopped for a moment, on business.

"Miss Scott has sent me word that she is too ill to be out to-morrow, and wishes me to try to supply a teacher for her class. I hardly know where to look for one; can you suggest a suitable person? We must not have *that* class neglected!"

Miss Lynde shook her head in a doubtful way; then her face brightened, and she said: "I can lend you this scholar of mine, if you will persuade her to undertake the charge."

"I? Why, Miss Lynde! How can you think of such a thing! I am not fit for a teacher!"

"You are accustomed to little ones, and know their ways. Miss Scott has the Infant Class, you know; I really think, Eunice dear, that you would manage it very well."

"But my eyes!" remonstrated Eunice. I cannot read, their lessons; or *ought* not to!" she added, blushing as she thought she detected a twinkle of fun in the glance of her friend.

"Miss Scott is merely drilling these little ones upon the Lord's Prayer, and the Creed, at present," said Mr. Robertson; "you could teach those without eyes:—then they sing some little hymns, which you can omit, if they are not familiar to you; but you can easily occupy the time, and interest them, by telling them some Bible story, or talking to them.

"I shall be very glad, if you will attend to the class to-morrow, Miss Eunice. I do not want those little ones to become scattered, or disaffected;—if you will try to interest them to-morrow, we will hope Miss Scott will be able to resume her charge by another Sunday."

Eunice at length consented, though with a good deal of reluctance, to undertake the class, provided Mr. Robertson failed to find some one more experienced.

It is my belief that the reverend gentleman did not exert himself very much in the matter. He was satisfied, from Miss Lynde's manner, that Eunice could do what he wanted; and that it would be a good thing for her.

After he had gone, Eunice looked reproachfully at her friend.

"How *could* you, Miss Lynde? Just think
how embarrassed I shall feel! And then I
must be absent from your class, too!"

"Well, my dear, I thought you wanted something to do for the Master;—a little piece of
Lenten work!"

Eunice could not reply to this remark, and
the smile which accompanied it.

Eunice did find herself rather embarrassed
when she was ushered into the separate room
used by the Infant Class, and met the gaze of
some twenty pair of roguish eyes.

But very soon she contrived to fix their attention upon the lesson, and became really
interested in drawing out their answers.

At the first pause, one little fellow shouted:

"Now, teacher, can't we sing?"

"I am afraid I do not know your hymns,"
replied Eunice; "what would you *like* to
sing?"

"Let us sing

'Jesus, high in glory?'"

Eunice happened to know the hymn, which she had often sung with the little ones at home.

She knew that they were accustomed to the same tune, for she had often heard them singing, while in her own class.

She hesitated a moment, but the children were eagerly watching for her to begin, so she started the hymn, and went on with confidence as she found herself supported at once by a chorus of infant voices.

Miss Lynde heard the strain, as she was engaged in her own duties; and smiled to herself at the success of her scheme.

Miss Scott was not able to be out the next Sunday, nor for two or three weeks afterward; and Eunice became very much interested in her new work, and proved quite an efficient substitute.

CHAPTER XI.

Anxious Days.

"Parts of a chord, whose harmonies
Yield to the Master's hand alone,
As, with attentive ear, He tries
Note after note, till all are one."

HE eyes were gaining;—yes, they were certainly stronger! Eunice was allowed to use them, in a good light, for half an hour at a time; and when no ill effects resulted, her friends congratulated her upon the restoration of her old privileges.

"But you must be very careful, my dear child; a very little imprudence might deprive you again of the use of your eyes, and subject you to all this suffering and annoyance once more."

Eunice assented to her aunt's observation,

(139)

feeling happy enough to promise any amount of caution.

She was not to resume her drawing lessons yet; that was hardly safe; indeed, as there now wanted but three weeks to Easter, it would have been scarcely worth while.

Not much was said in allusion to her return home, but Eunice felt that she ought to go soon after Easter.

To her other studies she applied herself with great diligence; and her music lessons now well deserved the name, for she was becoming well grounded in the rudiments of the science, and improving her voice and taste, as well. Miss Lynde was not one to do things by halves.

"A letter from Mansfield! Who speaks first?" said Mr. Hartwell, holding up the missive, as he entered the family room.

"Why, I had one yesterday!" exclaimed Eunice, stretching out a hand for it, nevertheless.

It was but a brief note, saying that two of the children were taken ill the day before its date, and the physician pronounced their attack to be scarlet-fever.

The rest of the family had been exposed; and Mrs. Somers evidently wrote in all the anxiety which the appearance of that dreaded malady is sure to awaken.

"We will write again to-morrow," the letter concluded; "by which time we can better judge how the fever will go with them."

Eunice was almost in a fever herself with impatient anxiety for the next tidings, and her aunt was scarcely less anxious.

The next letter was not received until the second day after: it was but a line, from Mr. Somers, to say that the children, Ranney and Bess, were very ill indeed.

"Oh, auntie!" exclaimed Eunice, with tearful excitement, "I *must* go home at once, to help mother take care of them!"

"No, my dear child; I knew of course that you would wish to go, if we had no more cheerful tidings to-day, and your uncle and I have talked it all over.

"Your uncle has seen Dr. Williams, and he

quite agrees with us that there would be a good
deal of danger in exposing you to scarlet-fever
in the present state of your eyes. I think, too,
your mother would not wish you to come home;
—she will be thankful to feel that one child has
escaped the infection. So, my dear, I am going
to Mansfield, myself, to stay with your mother
until the children are well again, which we will
hope may be very soon."

"But, auntie, you may take the fever yourself! Oh, I do think I ought to go!"

"I shall not be likely to take it, my love, and
we are quite sure that this is the best plan.
Your part will be to help Aunt Dora with the
housekeeping, and in taking care of Aunt
Mildred, while I am gone. And you must keep
a cheerful face, to make sunshine for Uncle
Ransom when he comes home, so that he will
not miss me too much."

Eunice could not reply at once. She felt, as
she would have expressed it, all in a whirl;
but Aunt Edith's next remark brought her to
herself:—

"I want to get off this afternoon, if possible;

so come, my dear! I shall need to keep you busy every moment."

It was well for Eunice that she had not much time to reflect upon the fact that Aunt Edith was really going to her home; and that the children were dangerously ill, and she must not go to them.

"Now, Eunice dear," said Aunt Edith, the while methodically sorting from her drawers the articles which she would need for her journey, "I have not asked much help of you in the way of household duties this winter; but I don't think you have forgotten your domestic accomplishments; and I must depend upon you to take charge of some things while I am gone."

"I'm sure I shall be glad to, auntie; I feel as if I ought to work all the time, as hard as I can!"

"There is no need of that, dear, and I think you will have plenty of time for study. But I want you to take care of my china closet; as I do, every morning, you know. Aunt Dora will have quite too much to do to attend to that, and I should not like the nice china and silver taken into the kitchen.   And I want you to take charge of the library, too; and keep it nicely dusted and in order."

"Is that all, Aunt Edith? Can't you give me something more to do?"

"That is all that I want to depend upon you for, my dear. To do these things well will require considerable time and care. But I dare say Aunt Dora will be glad of your help, every day, in various ways: I think you will be able to help her most by staying with Aunt Mildred occasionally. You could wait upon her very handily; and I know she likes very much to have you with her."

Again Eunice felt herself reproved, on this point. She *might* have devoted a little more time and attention to the invalid, who had been so very kind to her.

Mrs. Hartwell started by the afternoon train. After she had left the house, Eunice tried to recall her wandering thoughts, and attend to her lessons, but she succeeded but poorly.

At her recitation hour, she was obliged to

confess that she had not prepared much of a lesson.

"This has been a very busy day," said Mr. Hartwell; "you are very excusable, my dear."

"I had time enough, after auntie was gone," said Eunice, truthfully; "but—but I couldn't seem to fix my mind on anything!"

Mr. Hartwell observed the tears which *would* start, and said, kindly:

"My dear child, you have a new lesson of patient trust to learn now. You must try to trust the dear absent ones to their Heavenly Father's love, and not be too anxious about them. If I thought it were best for you, I would permit you to lay aside your studies, through this time of trial. But do you not think it would be much better to go calmly on with your accustomed duties, than to sit with folded hands and tearful eyes, waiting for tidings?"

"I suppose it would, uncle; and I really will try."

Miss Dora called Eunice at an earlier hour than usual, the next morning.

"Come, my dear! If you are to be assistant housekeeper, you must spring up in good season, or you will not be ready for church."

"Why, Aunt Dora! I can't go to church this morning; I have to wash the breakfast things, you know, and I shall not be ready!"

"Yes, you can, dear, by being prompt, and having everything ready in your room before breakfast. Your Aunt Edith managed it, you know. If there was a little extra to be done, she attended to it after she came home."

"I'm not so smart as Aunt Edith!" rejoined Eunice, in not the most pleasant of tones; but the words and the tone were lost upon the busy monitor, who was on her way down-stairs.

"I don't see," murmured the girl, as she began to dress, "how I can do my housework, and study, and go to church, too! I don't think it is my duty to try!"

But that word 'duty' struck a chord which kept on vibrating, to her great disturbance.

That sermon of Mr. Robertson's, at the beginning of Lent; it had not before crossed

Eunice, in her purposes and plans; but now it would recur to her mind.

His text had been: "Ye shall go and pray unto me, and I will hearken unto you."

He had dwelt especially upon the duty of 'going'—stepping out of the routine even of necessary work,—to join in the prayers and devotions of the Church, at this season.

Heretofore it had been very pleasant for Eunice to attend the eight o'clock service; being quite at leisure afterward to walk home with Rhoda, or with Miss Lynde; in fact, she had chosen this time, directly after church, for her musical practice, twice a week, or sometimes oftener.

But now she would be obliged to come directly home, and finish her morning duties, taking some time later in the day for her other calls abroad.

Eunice's reflections upon the sermon changed her views as to the matter of duty, before she was ready to go down-stairs. She came to the conclusion that one could hardly be said to "search for the Lord with all the heart," who went to the services only when it was perfectly convenient.

"That is right, my love!" said Miss Dora, seeing Eunice emerge from her room as the bell began to ring, all ready for church.

"You see I cannot put my own doctrines in practice this morning; I cannot leave my poor sister, to go to church."

"Is Aunt Mildred feeling more poorly than usual?" asked Eunice.

"Yes, I am afraid she is; she had quite a faint turn just now."

"Well, Aunt Dora, I will come directly home after church, and perhaps I can help you take care of her."

"Are you coming home with me to practice this morning?" asked Miss Lynde, after church.

Eunice explained her additional home duties, and added: "I should like to come at one o'clock, if you will be at leisure then; that is, I will try to, if I can be spared."

"Very well, dear; I will expect you punctually at one, if you can come. I dare say you will find yourself quite busy while your aunt is away, and I am glad to see you are taking up the new duties so cheerfully!"

Mrs. Ellett was hardly fit to be left alone, that morning; and when Eunice had dusted the library, and was ready to study, she proposed to take her books up and sit with her, to be ready if anything was needed.

"Well, if you will, my dear, I shall be very glad; for I ought to go down-stairs awhile to attend to things."

Not much chance had Eunice to study, however; the good lady, in the first place, was very glad to see her, for a little talk about the news from her home, and so on.

Then, when Eunice had settled herself by the window, with her books, the interruptions were very frequent.

Mrs. Ellett, being really in a nervous and suffering condition, seemed quite to forget that she was trying to prepare her lessons, and required one little service, and then another, to the great hindrance of the student.

At last she laid aside her books, and remained beside the invalid, bathing her head, and trying to amuse and cheer her, until Miss Dora came up.

"Now, Eunie, I will stay here; you can go and finish your lessons."

"Ah! I'm afraid I have hindered you, dearie;" said Aunt Mildred; "but you have been a real comfort to me;—thank you, my child!"

Only half an hour to study; then she must run down to Miss Lynde's for a short practice; then back again to her lessons.

The reading with Aunt Dora had been given up, when Eunice was permitted to use her eyes once more.

"You will do better now to read at your own time, and in your own 'closet,' my love," Miss Dora had said.

If Eunice was tempted to overlook or slight her private devotions, while she remained at her uncle's, an occasional glimpse of Aunt Dora stealing away from her pressing occupations for her few moments of refreshment, reminded her of the neglected duty.

The day above described was a fair specimen of the next two weeks, except that, some days, Mrs. Ellett was even more poorly, requiring constant nursing; and that more than once Eunice was obliged to give up her singing lesson.

Mrs. Hartwell, or Mrs. Somers herself, wrote frequently.

Bess was decidedly better; Ranney was over the fever, but the letters alluded in rather doubtful terms to him; George had taken his turn, and was very sick for a few days; and, at the last account, the two little ones were taken down.

The Collect for the Fifth Sunday in Lent was a comfort to Eunice through these busy, anxious days: it was, as she said to Miss Lynde, so much like the one for the Second Sunday.

That had expressed so well her own personal wants; but now she used the seasonable words to plead for the dear ones who were laid low, and it was such a comfort to feel that, in soul and body, they were in the hands of the Lord.

CHAPTER XII.

A Memorable Week.

"When our heads are bowed with woe,
When our bitter tears o'erflow ;
When we mourn the lost and dear,
Jesu, Son of Mary, hear!

" Thou hast bowed the dying head,
Thou the blood of life hast shed,
Thou hast filled a mortal bier ;
Jesu, Son of Mary, hear!"

THE Holy Week of our Saviour's Passion and death had begun.

Miss Scott, the teacher of the Infant Class, was present on the Sunday morning, and Eunice was relieved from her charge, and able to resume her place with her old classmates, and to listen to their teacher's earnest comment upon " the example of His patience."

Once, while Miss Lynde was speaking, Eunice glanced at Rhoda. She was listening, with the calm, restful look which grew more and more habitual to her.

"*She* is following the example of His patience," thought her friend; "oh, I wish *I* might, as truly!"

Be of good cheer, young Christian; you are learning, as Rhoda said, in the same school: the lessons of the past few weeks shall not prove to have been given in vain!

Services were appointed for the evenings of this week, as well as the mornings; and Eunice requested that she might give up her lessons, for the week.

"If you would like to go to the evening services, Eunice, I shall be at home each evening to go with you;" said Dick.

"Thank you, cousin; I want to go when I can, but I think I ought to take turns with Aunt Dora, this week, in staying with Aunt Mildred."

"Well, then, I must go all the more regularly, as your proxy; and I may be useful in escorting Miss Dora, in her turn!"

Mr. Hartwell expected to attend the evening

services himself; but he was very glad to hear Dick's offer, and to perceive that, under cover of taking care of Eunice, there existed a good resolve of his own.

Wednesday brought sad tidings. A telegram was received, announcing that Baby Walter was dead.

Eunice was at first almost stunned by this news. Her anxieties had reached to the probable suffering of the children at home, and the care and exhaustion of the parents, but she had scarcely entertained the thought of death.

And could it be that he was gone—the bright, merry baby boy, whom she had dearly loved! That she should never again have opportunity to tend and please him, and make amends for the grudging manner in which, as she bitterly remembered now, those little ministries had been too often performed!

Eunice felt as if she must go home, to take one parting look at her dear little brother, and follow him to the grave. But her uncle, who had brought home the telegram, and waited to soothe the sobbing mourner, kindly, but firmly shook his head, at the first mention of this.

"No, my daughter, it would not be right to run the risk; do not think of it!

"Follow him in your thoughts, dear child,— follow the happy infant spirit to the Paradise whither angels have borne it, and where there shall be no more pain."

As Eunice still sobbed, almost convulsively, he bent over and kissed her forehead.

"Eunice dear, the teachings of this week will help you to bear this sad trial, I know.

"Think of Him who 'became obedient unto death;'—think of the words we have just heard read this morning: 'Not my will, but Thine be done!'—Remember the example of His patience."

Aye, indeed! Mr. Hartwell could not have chosen his words more wisely to hush the tumult of grief and regret.

As he stood beside Eunice, waiting, a few moments, she struggled for composure, and raising her head presently, said in a quiet tone, "Thank you, dear uncle."

He knew that he might safely leave her, then. In a little time, Eunice went up to Mrs. Ellett's room, and offered to release Miss Dora, who had been occupied very closely through the morning, in the sick-room.

"My dear!" remonstrated Miss Dora, in a low tone, "it will be too much for you to-day, I am afraid; do not try, if you would rather be alone."

"I think it will be better for me to be trying to help some one else," replied Eunice, with a faint smile.

Miss Dora looked in her face a moment, and then said:

"I see! The Lord is teaching you how to bear this trouble," and left her with her charge.

Eunice had no reason to regret this effort on her part.

Aunt Mildred had lost all her own children in early infancy, and she knew how to comfort the bereaved sister. She seemed, in turn, to forget her own suffering in sympathy with Eunice; and she spoke so sweetly of the ransomed little ones in Paradise, of their safety, and secured bliss, that Eunice felt she would not wish him back to this troubled world again.

Miss Lynde heard of the little one's death, and came in the afternoon to offer her friendly sympathy.

The next day there were letters; one for Eunice from her mother. She knew it must have been written very soon after the baby's death, and felt gratefully how like her unselfish mother it was to remember the grief of her absent one, in the midst of her own fresh sorrow.

The other letter was from Mrs. Hartwell to her husband. He read it, glanced at Eunice, and then, on second thought, placed it in his pocket-book for another time.

It was not until the afternoon of Good Friday, that, after consultation with his sisters, he called Eunice into the library.

"My dear, I do not know that Aunt Edith quite intended this letter for your perusal; but as its subject very nearly concerns you, we think it better that you should read just what she says, yourself." And he gave the letter into her hand.

"You will have received, ere this," so the letter began, "the tidings of the death of sister's youngest darling.

"You and I, love, know very well what the trial is. Madeline and her husband bear it with Christian calmness, as we would expect of their long-tried faith.

"George and Bessie are doing very well, only needing care to avoid the danger of taking cold. Little Susy has had the disease much more lightly than the other children. But I feel anxious about Ranney, your namesake, you know.

"He is entirely free from the fever, but it appears he has never been really well since the fall which sister mentioned, some weeks since.

"Very likely the attack of fever has aggravated his previous ailments; but, whatever the cause, the child is far from well. He complains of feeling 'so tired,' most of the time; and seems to have a good deal of pain at intervals.

"I should like very much to bring him home with me, for the change of air, and to obtain the advice of our physicians in Holmeford in his case.

"I think his parents would entrust him to me, for, if he has sustained some internal injury, which is my fear, he should be treated accordingly, without delay.

"But I know that I shall be very fully occupied when I return home. Poor sister Mildred, from your account, must need Dora's constant care; and there is all the spring work, and the guests whom you expect soon.

"I see but one way to manage it. If Eunice were to stay with us, and devote herself to the care of her brother, I could very well give him the general oversight required.

"But, between us, Eunice was never remarkably patient with this little fellow; and now his merry mischief of former days has given place to a peevishness and irritability, which would be much more trying to her patience.

"What do you think best? I shall only await your decision and reply to return home, as there is no farther especial reason for my remaining here."

Eunice read the letter through with evident emotion; and tearfully exclaimed:

"Oh, Uncle Ransom! You *know* I will do everything I can for Ranney! May he come? Will you write at once?"

"I will telegraph, my dear, if you are sure you realize what you are undertaking.

"It is not only that your auntie will have a great deal to do, after her return; I know very well that she will find herself very much fatigued and worn, after the care of the past three weeks, and I should hardly consent to have her continue the care of a sick child, in addition to her home duties.

"*That* must devolve almost entirely upon you, if he comes: do you think you can stand the care and confinement, and the giving up of your own pursuits, in great measure?"

"I don't wonder you doubt me, uncle," replied Eunice, humbly; "but I do very much wish to try!

"It seems," she added, after a little pause,

"as if God gave me this opportunity to show how sorry I am."

The message was sent at once; and Eunice, hopeful for her little brother, thankful that she was to be called to minister to him; and comforted concerning the dear ones at home, and the darling whom God had taken, prepared for a blessed and happy Easter.

But this week, so fraught already with lessons for a life-time, was to be marked by one more event.

It was towards evening, on Saturday, that Frances Lynde called at the house, to seek for Eunice.

When ushered into the parlor she found Dick North there, he having returned earlier than usual, and a little before the hour for dinner.

"O Dick! she exclaimed, on seeing him, "I have come with more distressing tidings for that poor child. How shall I tell her?"

"You do not mean—is it possible that that little friend of hers is gone?"

"Rhoda Merritt; yes! I did not know that

you knew anything about her; she died suddenly, this morning."

Here Eunice entered, and Dick hastily retreated, more moved than he wished to show, himself, and unwilling to witness his young cousin's sorrow.

Miss Lynde drew Eunice to a seat beside her, and threw her arms around her.

"My darling girl, can you bear to hear of another bereavement?"

Eunice gazed wonderingly in the face of her friend, and perceiving that she had been weeping, the truth flashed upon her mind.

"Is it Rhoda?" she asked, in a quiet tone, yet trembling,—almost shuddering, as she spoke.

"It is, dear; the call which she has so long expected, has come, and we believe that it found her watching."

"'Blessed are those servants,'" Eunice began; but her voice broke, and she could not finish the quotation.

"Yes, indeed! We cannot know now *how* blessed," rejoined Miss Lynde.

Then, knowing that Eunice wished to hear all, she went on :

"It was this morning, dear : you know that she was at church yesterday, in the morning; shall we ever forget that sweet, placid expression of her face as we saw her then ?

"She awoke this morning feeling distressed, it seems. The pain passed off, but she evidently regarded it as premonitory, and spoke of it thus to her friends.

"She lay on the lounge, as her mother desired, although she felt better after breakfast.

"Her mother did not leave her, and her father felt too anxious to remain long from the house. They were both with her when the sudden attack came on which speedily wrought the change.

"I have just come from the house. O Eunice, there is no bitterness in that death !"

Eunice was weeping, but quietly.

"It is Easter Even," she said.

"Yes; the day of all others that she, dear child of the Church as she was, would have

chosen, for her friends to stand around her
mortal remains. I thought of the lines :

> " ' Go to the grave ; for there thy Saviour lay
>   In death's embraces, ere He rose on high :
> And all the ransomed, by that narrow way
>   Pass to eternal life, beyond the sky.

> " ' Go to the grave : no, take thy flight above ;
>   Be thy pure spirit present with the Lord :—
> Where thou for faith and hope hast perfect love,
>   And open vision, for the written word !' "

It was a blessed, happy Easter, not to Eunice
alone, but to all who knew and loved the dear
young Christian who had been taken from their
midst.

Every word of the glorious Easter service
spoke hope and comfort to their hearts, and
forbade them to mourn.

The service of the afternoon was especially
for the Sunday-school ; one for which they had
been preparing for some time. Mr. Robertson
took the fitting occasion to speak to the hearts
of the children, of the hope, the glorious hope
which had sustained and cheered their young
companion ; so long face to face, as it were,
with death.

The funeral was appointed for Easter Tuesday; and it was largely attended by the members of the Sunday-school and congregation.

Eunice went to the house, more than once, in the interval, to stand beside her dear young friend, and gaze upon the sweet face, wearing such a happy smile.

"You must come often to see us," said the bereaved mother, "when our darling is borne away from us; she loved you very dearly!"

CHAPTER XIII.

Journey.

"But when the self-abhorring thrill
Is passed, as pass it must;
When tasks of life thy spirit fill,
Risen from thy tears and dust;
Then be the self-renouncing will
The seal of thy calm trust!"

HE next day, Wednesday, a week from the day of baby Walter's death, Aunt Edith arrived, with her charge.

Eunice was shocked at the change in her little brother, who looked pale and thin and listless,—very different from the merry, roguish child from whom she had parted in the autumn.

He was tired with his journey, Aunt Edith explained; it had seemed to fatigue him more than she anticipated, although she had arranged

(166)

EUNICE AND RANNEY.—PAGE 167.

her shawls as a pillow, that he might lie down a good part of the time.

It was late in the afternoon when they arrived.

"Now, my little boy," said Aunt Edith, "would you like to go right to bed, and rest; and have some dinner brought up to you, by-and-by?"

"No, ma'am; I'd rather stay and see Eunie."

"Very well, then," his aunt answered, smiling; "I'll go and dispose of my goods and chattels, and leave you in her charge."

"We'll sit on the sofa, Ranney, and you shall lay your head on me, and rest in that way;—so. Dear little fellow! You must make. haste and get well; sister don't like to see you looking so poorly."

"Then you don't 'hate' me, Eunie?" said the child, scanning her face.

"*Hate* you? No! I love you dearly!" said Eunice, stooping to kiss him.

How the question hurt her. Was it possible that he had treasured up those hasty words in his memory until this time.

The next day a physician of some eminence was called in, to give his advice in the case.

He of course could not form a decided opinion until he had observed the child for some little time ; but, from what Mrs. Hartwell was able to tell him of his symptoms, he agreed with her, and, indeed, with the old family physician in Mansfield, in judging that there had been some spinal injury resulting from his fall, though he hoped it was slight, and would yield to treatment.

He could not determine, at first sight, how much of his present feebleness was due to the recent illness.

In reply to Mr. Hartwell's inquiries as to the physician's opinion, that evening, his wife answered :

"As far as I could gather from what he said, he seemed to agree pretty much with old Phillis."

"Who is she?"

"A nice old colored woman whom sister has had to help her, whenever she needed help ;— or, more correctly, when she felt that she could afford to hire it.

"She is very fond of the children, and has kept an anxious eye upon Ranney of late.

"She seemed very much pleased to hear that I was to bring him to Holmeford, to see what could be done for him.

"'I'm right glad, missis!' said she; 'it's high time that child was seed to! He hasn't been like himself since that time he fell off the ladder. It's my belief that he *hurted the spine of his back,* more or less!'"

"Well, we must have Dr. Browne give his close attention to the case; and, if he desires, consult with other physicians. We will spare no expense or effort to save the little fellow from a life of suffering. He seems a very pleasant child!"

"He is; though, as Phillis said, he is not like himself now: I never saw a more bright, intelligent child, for his years."

Ranney was of course amused and interested with the novelty of all about him, having never been in a large town before, and, after resting from the journey, he appeared brighter and better from this cause.

To Eunice he seemed very dear and loveable.
Divested of the mischievousness of his healthy
days, and as yet showing no signs of the fret-
fulness which his aunt had remarked upon, she
wondered that the latter should have fancied it
would be such a trial to her temper and
patience to take care of him.

She had made most determined resolves that
her whole time, if necessary, should be given
up to him; and that no unreasonableness or
peevishness on his part should betray her into
anger or impatience.

Eunice had not as yet resumed her studies,
which she laid aside at the commencement of
Passion-week; her mind this week had been
fully occupied;—at first with the funeral of her
friend Rhoda, then with the-arrival of her aunt
and Ranney, and subsequently in arranging
for the comfort of the little invalid, and
preparing to carry out his physician's directions.

But at dinner on Saturday Mr. Hartwell
observed :

"We have had a long vacation, daughter;

but I suppose our routine will begin again on
Monday ; say you not so ?"

Eunice glanced with some surprise from her
uncle to Ranney, who was beside her at table.

" I hardly supposed I should be able to
study much now," she replied.

" O yes! I think so ;" interposed Aunt
Edith ; " at least we will hope you can, as a
general thing."

She checked the remark Eunice was about to
make, by a significant look ;—but after Ranney
was asleep that evening, the subject was
resumed.

" Eunice, my love, I see you are inclined to
be very faithful and devoted to your boy, but
you must not *over-do* the matter.

" We must try, as the doctor says, to keep
him amused and happy, but still it would
hardly be well to let him feel that you must do
nothing but wait upon him. We must not
make a tyrant of our little boy!

" Unless Ranney should grow worse, instead
of better, as we hope, I think you will be able
to go on with your usual studies; keeping

him with you, perhaps, when we are too busy to watch him.

"I would be glad to take charge of him during your study hours, for I am aware you may find it difficult, sometimes, to prepare your lessons. But you know, dear, that I shall be very busy now, and must leave him mostly upon your hands.

"You will have plenty of opportunities for the exercise of patience, in trying to carry on your studies, subject to constant interruption ; but it may be a good discipline for you, my love.

" Try to feel content with *doing what you can*, always taking first ' the duty which lies nearest you ;' and you will have learned a most valuable lesson to help you in your life-work !"

Aunt Edith's words were accompanied with a smile of kindly meaning, which Eunice well understood.

How strange it seemed to her, that the very path she had so longed to escape, while at home—the path

"Where *duties* fence life's narrow ground."

now opened plainly before her again amid the

very scenes where she had fondly hoped to press on joyfully in the ways of her own choice!

Still musing thus, she retired to her own room for the night; and bending over her little brother, her charge by night as well as by day, she kissed him, as he quietly slept—then smiled through her tears as she murmured:

"Dear Rhoda! Yes, it is 'a school,' indeed! and oh! how glad I am that it is 'the same!'"

The young disciple had begun to understand that it was no hard taskmaster, but her faithful Teacher, and Heavenly Guide, who set before her this lesson to be humbly learned.

In the psalm which Eunice read, before undressing, were these words, which well expressed her heart's desire at that hour:

"Show me Thy ways, O Lord :
Teach me Thy paths :
Lead me in Thy truth and teach me,
For Thou art the God of my salvation :
On Thee do I wait all the day."

The next morning was Sunday, and Eunice awoke wondering whether she should be able to go to church that day. She had not left Ranney yet, but a few moments at a time; and besides, she did not wish to have any one else detained to take care of him ;—and the church was at rather too great a distance for him to walk.

The doctor wished him to walk but very little, but to take gentle exercise in any other way that could be devised.

Aunt Mildred, aware of this, had declared herself quite equal to a drive, the day previous, and ordered a hack ; taking Eunice and Ranney with her.

Ranney was sleeping so soundly when his sister was ready to go down-stairs, that she would not disturb him, but softly quitted the room.

In passing through the hall, she fancied she heard Mrs. Ellett call, and went in to see if she wanted anything.

"I did not call, dearie, but I am as glad to see my sunbeam as if I had!"

Eunice gave the dear old lady an affectionate kiss, and inquired after her health.

"I feel better than I have in some time, my love; really, the drive yesterday must have done me good: I hardly supposed, when I ordered the hack, that I should go, but I thought our little boy could enjoy it, whether I did or not."

"You are very kind, Aunt Mildred; as you always are!"

"Ah! I am afraid I have seemed a poor selfish old woman, of late, my dear! But you have been very patient, as have all my friends; and I am so thankful to feel a little better now; for I think I may help you some with your dear little boy. And, by the way, do you think he will like to stay with me, while you go to Church to-day?"

"Oh, I am afraid it will tire you to have him here, Aunt Mildred!"

"No, my dear, I think not; and we grew pretty good friends yesterday. I fancy he will be happy with me. Jenny will be about the house, and I can ring if I need anything: I think we two invalids can take care of each other this morning; and your Aunt Dora will be at home this afternoon, probably."

"Well, aunty, I will see what Ranney thinks about it; I shall be very glad to go!"

Ranney was disposed to act a little babyish, and cling to Eunice; but a timely word from his Aunt Edith made him a little ashamed, and he made no further objection.

When Eunice returned after the morning service, she found the little fellow very contented and happy. "He had a nice time," he said; and he seemed quite willing to spare his sister again.

Thus a precedent was happily established for the Sundays.

But this was a favorable specimen of Ranney's days. They were not all so bright. At times he seemed to suffer a good deal, and was very irritable and exacting.

Then the physician's directions were such as to require a good deal of time and careful attention. Mrs. Hartwell intended to administer the strengthening baths, and the frequent rubbing herself; but the child preferred to be tended by his sister, and Eunice begged to do it, promising to be very careful in following instructions, and guarding against exposure to cold.

Once she came near losing Ranney's confidence entirely. She had prepared a warm salt bath, and being a little absent-minded, made it rather more than warm.

Helping the little boy to spring into the tub, she was startled by his scream of pain, and quickly caught him out again.

Ranney surveyed his little par-boiled toes with an injured and indignant look; but Eunice was so full of self-reproach for her carelessness, and begged his forgiveness so heartily, that his mood quickly changed.

"Never mind, Eunie!" said he; "it didn't hurt much! You wont make it too hot again, will you?"

She never did.

A letter from Eunice to her mother, written after Ranney had been nearly two weeks in Holmeford, may best describe the condition of things at this time.

"HOLMEFORD, *April* 28.

"I know you wish to hear often, mother dear, from your *two* 'absent darlings,' so I write again, although it is but a day or two since

Aunt Edith sent you a full account of the treatment which Dr. Browne had prescribed for Ranney.

"Dear little fellow! It is sad to think what a time it may be, and I suppose, *must* be, before he can be well and strong again; and yet it is a comfort to know that there is so much that may be done to help him, and prevent his growing very much worse.

"He is very patient, I think: when he is fretful it is very plain that he is suffering and cannot help it. We get along very nicely together.

"You ask if my studies are at an end, for the present.

"Oh, no! I manage to prepare my lessons for uncle, every day; and auntie and I do not often miss our readings.

"Ranney sits with me while I study, and amuses himself quietly, unless he is feeling very poorly. There are a number of books with handsome engravings, in the library, which please him; and I have found out that he begins to read quite nicely, though we do not like to have him read much at a time : I read aloud to him, a good deal.

"My singing lessons are at a stand-still, for I cannot leave Ranney to go to Miss Lynde ; and, of course, I have not resumed my drawing ;— I doubt if I ever shall.

"I have not been to see dear Rhoda's mother since the funeral, but I hope to be able to get there soon : you know Dr. Browne does not wish Ranney to walk much ; if it were not for that, I could take him with me.

"But do not think that I mean to complain of these things, darling mother! I am glad to give up something for Ranney's sake ; and I am very happy in taking care of him.

"We mean to take Ranney out, in some way, every pleasant day. Uncle says he will see to it, for he must have the air; but I know it costs a good deal to hire a horse; and Aunt Mildred has been *so* kind.

"She has proposed a drive, several mornings, though she was only able to go herself twice : the other times she laughed and said, 'Ranney must get the benefit of the drive for *both*, for her courage failed!' ᾿I knew very well that she ordered the hack on purpose for him.

"Two mornings Uncle Ransom came himself, with a buggy, and said there was plenty of room for me, with Ranney. Those were delightful drives : uncle is so kind and pleasant.

"Then, yesterday, we had the funniest ride of all. Cousin Dick proposed that we should go, right after breakfast, so that he could help us, and take a ride in the street cars, out to the end of the route : there are two lines of street cars in Holmeford now, and one passes the store where Cousin Dick is.

"He carried Ranney, in his arms, to the car, and told us to stop at the store, when we came back, and he would carry him home.

"Wasn't that kind?—Ranney enjoyed the trip very much, and Cousin Dick says we must try it again.

"But I am making out a very long letter, and my boy is growing impatient ; so I must only send a loving kiss for papa and yourself, George and the little ones. I *do* want to see you all once more !   EUNICE."

We must give but a brief extract from the reply to this letter:

"I cannot tell you, dear daughter, what a relief and comfort this arrangement has been to me, although I sadly miss my boy, and it is rather hard for us to have our Eunice's absence indefinitely prolonged.

"I could see that our good old Dr. Wayne did not understand Ranney's case, or at least, was not skilful in its treatment. I longed for the advice which might save him from years of suffering, and perhaps deformity, but could not see how we were to obtain it.

"We owe a great deal of gratitude to your kind aunt and uncle, for devising the present plan; and we are grateful, too, to our dear child, for her cheerful acceptance of her part of the burden, without which it could scarcely have been undertaken.

"God bless and keep both our dear absent ones, and restore them to us in His own good time!"

CHAPTER XIV.

Incidents by the Way.

"Who from these children's steps, the thorns
  Of grief, and doubt, and care,
  Can kindly take ; or, for their peace,
  As kindly plant them there :

"Through regions sad with weeping storms,
  Dark wood, and frowning hill,
  Or valley, bright as angel's dreams,
  Can guide them, at His will."

"UNICE, I have a sentence to pronounce upon you!" said Mrs. Hartwell, at lunch, a day or two after.

"You are to run up-stairs at once, and dress: then disappear out of the front door, and not let me see you again until dinner-time!"

Ranney had been out, riding, and when he returned, had fallen asleep on the lounge in Mrs. Ellett's room, and was having a good nap.

"He will feel quite bright, when he awakes," said Aunt Edith, "and I can take care of him this afternoon. You have been too much confined since I came home, and I must see that you have a little more freedom, after this."

"I am sure, dear auntie, you need not worry about me; I have had a ride, almost every day, and have been to church both Sundays!"

"Yes, yes! but you want a good run, and a little time to yourself;—be off, now, and make the most of your liberty!"

Eunice was delighted to obey this command, and was soon in the street, on her way to Miss Lynde's.

On second thoughts she resolved to make sure of a call at Mrs. Merritt's, first; lest something should interfere with her purpose of going there.

Rhoda's mother affectionately welcomed her daughter's friend, and the two had a long and comforting talk, about the dear departed one.

Mrs. Merritt had long schooled herself to contemplate the thought of parting with her dear child, having had reason to believe that the separation might come at any time; and her grief was subdued, and her manner resigned, and even cheerful. The same trusting faith which had upheld the daughter, now sustained her parents under their bereavement.

Mrs. Merritt was much interested in hearing of Ranney, and was still inquiring about him, when her little boy, Jack, as he was usually called, entered, in search of his mother.

Mrs. Merritt had just mentioned that Jack seemed to feel his sister's death even more keenly than the two older boys, who were nearer her age: they attended school, and had not been quite as much with her, of late, which perhaps accounted for the seeming difference; but poor little Jack had depended very much upon 'sister Rhoda,' and he was, besides, of a very susceptible temperament, and grieved sadly over his loss.

Eunice greeted the child, as he came up; at first he did not seem inclined to respond, but some recollection crossed his mind, evidently, of the intimacy between Eunice and his sister, for he turned suddenly, and gave her his hand, and even returned her kiss.

Eunice drew him to a seat beside her, and said :

"I have not seen you in a good many days, Jack ; shall I tell you why?—I have had a little sick brother to take care of, and I did not like to leave him long, for fear he would miss me, and feel homesick. Will not you and Arthur come round and see him? He would like to see you, and play with you, very much!"

"Why don't you bring him here?" asked Jack.

"Because the doctor will not let him walk so far."

"Can't he ride?"

"By the way, Eunice," interposed Mrs. Merritt, "is he too large to ride in a child's perambulator? We have a very strong one, put away in the attic, and it does seem to me that you might manage to make him very comfortable in it. Suppose we have it down, and see!—Is he larger than Jack?"

"O no, he is a little younger, and considerably smaller, I should judge."

"Well, Jack, go and ask Ann to bring it down."

Jack soon re-appeared, wheeling the vehicle into the room. Then he gathered himself into it to convince Eunice that Ranney could ride in it, very well.

"We can make a higher seat than that, very easily, so that he can dispose of his limbs with more comfort and elegance," said Mrs. Merritt, smiling. You will not mind wheeling him about in it, will you, dear? Any one would conclude that the child was unable to walk."

"O no!" exclaimed Eunice, earnestly; "I should not mind anything which would give him so much pleasure as I think this will."

"Dear child!" said Mrs. Merritt, "that is so like Rhoda! I do not wonder that you two were friends!"

"I know where you live!" said Jack: "shall I take the carriage round for you? and then I can see your brother."

"Eunice is not going directly home, my dear; perhaps you had better wait until morning;

then you can go, if she would like it, and stay awhile with Ranney."

So it was settled; and Eunice, after heartily thanking Jack, and his mother, too, for the proffered kindness, took her leave, and went to see Miss Lynde.

Happily the young lady was at home, having just come in from a walk.

"I am *so* glad you did not come a little sooner, and find me out, my dear!"

"So am I," returned Eunice, "for more reasons than one. I think I have found a way, now, to go on with my much-missed lessons; if you are not tired of teaching me, and if you will not object to having Ranney come with me."

And Eunice explained about the perambulator.

"I am very glad!" exclaimed Miss Frances. "I have missed my pupil and friend very much! I shall be delighted to have you bring Ranney, and I think I can find enough to amuse him, when he is here, so that he will not mind our music."

"I think there will be no difficulty in finding amusement for him," said Eunice, smiling, as she glanced around the pleasant parlor, which was a sort of museum, in itself.

"How old is Ranney?"

"Nearly eight; but he is rather small for his age: if he does not take a notion that the vehicle is too babyish, I think he will enjoy getting about in it, very much. It seems quite strongly made, and of course the top pushes back, out of the way."

"I should think it would do nicely, dear, if it do not prove rather heavy work for *you*:—you must not go too far with him."

"No; but I can use it to bring him around here. You will see us quite often, I warn you!"

"I hope I shall! And now you can stay and practice a little while, I know. Take off your things, and then sit down here a moment, first; for I have some good news to tell you."

"*More* good news?" exclaimed Eunice, quickly placing herself beside her friend.

"Yes, darling; the girls have all decided

now;—Celia and Kitty, as well as the rest of our class.—We are to have the comfort of seeing them all come forward to Confirmation, Sunday after next!"

"Oh, that *is* good news!" cried Eunice; "I am *so* glad, for them, and for *you*, too! I wonder"—Eunice checked herself, and asked, instead:

"Do you know of any others who will be confirmed?"

"Not positively; but we hope that several others will conclude to stand forth then on the Lord's side. I *did* hope," added Frances, after a pause, "that our cousin Dick would decide aright this time; but I fear he does not think much of the subject."

Eunice looked up, wistfully.

"I was thinking of him!" she said. "Dear Miss Lynde, I think he cares a good deal more than one would suppose. I do yet hope he will come forward!"

The shy manner of her little friend revealed to Frances that she had suspected the state of the case between herself and her so-called cousin.

She drew Eunice close to her, and gave her a loving kiss, as she replied:

"I hope so, too, darling! Now come and let us try that new anthem together!"

It was a fact, that Dick North was deeply attached to Frances; and that she could easily have returned the attachment, but for the one obstacle which caused her to keep a strict guard upon her affections. Dick was, as she believed, regardless of religious duties, living without God in the world: and Frances Lynde was not one to give her heart and hand into the keeping of such a man.

Ranney was very much pleased with his new conveyance, and also with the boy friends who came to bring it; for Arthur came too.

Arthur was "nearly as big as brother George," as Ranney confidentially informed him; and this led to an animated account of George's exploits, which, to the town-boys, was very amusing.

"It's most school-time," said Arthur; "I must be off! Shall I come, some time, and give you a ride in this thing? I'm stronger than your sister!"

Ranney was much pleased with the offer, and thought Arthur was a *real* nice fellow, "*most* as clever as Georgie!"

Little Jack stayed an hour or two with Ranney, which gave Eunice a capital chance to read up her Latin; and then she proposed that they should take Ranney out; which they did, and all enjoyed it.

One morning, when Eunice was studying, Ranney asked for a paper and pencil, and Eunice opened the drawer of the table in which her drawing materials and sketches were kept, to supply him.

"What is that, Eunie?" said he, pointing to one of her drawings.

She took it out, and showed it to him.

Mr. Hartwell was in the room; a very unusual thing at that time of the day, but he had been detained by some matters of business.

He looked up from his writing, and said:

"Eunice makes nice pictures, doesn't she, little man?"

"Yes, sir. Please make some more, Eunie; why don't you?"

"Oh, I don't have Mr. Neville to show me how," replied she, laughing.

"Shall we send her off to the picture-man, Ranney, to learn to make more pictures?

"Seriously, Eunice, you may as well be taking a few more lessons; your eyes are quite well again, are they not?"

"I think so, uncle; I should at least be glad to try;—but I do not know that I can leave Ranney, to take the lessons."

"Ho! Yes you can! I can stay up in Aunt Mildred's room when you go," quoth Ranney, who was quite interested in the *picture* making.

Mrs. Hartwell "wondered they had not thought of it before," and so it was settled that Eunice should re-commence the next day, which was the day the class met.

"Well, my dear," said her aunt, as she returned from her lesson, "what did Mr. Neville say to his truant pupil?"

"He seemed glad to have me begin again,

and he said we must work in earnest, to make up for lost time."

"Do not let yourself become so engrossed as to forget to be careful in using your eyes, my dear child! You will promise me to stop drawing at once, when you feel the least pain or weakness in them, will you not?"

"Indeed I will, Aunt Edith. I suppose I must expect some interruptions from them;— and there must probably be some days when I shall not be able to leave Ranney.

"I told Mr. Neville he must not be surprised if I should miss some lessons;—but I am *very* glad to be able to go on, Aunt Edith,—if only for half the time."

Eunice was greatly favored in being spared any further trouble with her eyes;—taught by past experience, she was very careful to work in a good light, and not too long at a time.

But her little charge sometimes interfered with her delightful work; Eunice soon discovered that it was harder to be patient when interrupted in the midst of her drawing, than at any other occupation; and she was obliged to keep a close watch over herself, to avoid breaking her resolution.

The day on which she was to have taken the third lesson, Ranney was feeling more than commonly unwell. It was a rainy day, and he had not been out, which perhaps aggravated his misery; and as the hour for the lesson drew near, Eunice saw, with much disappointment, . that there was little hope of her being able to go.

Mrs. Hartwell was very busy, and had evidently forgotten that it was "drawing day;" and Aunt Mildred had a " poor turn," as she would have described it, so Ranney could not stay with her.

There was nothing for it but resignation; so Eunice put away her drawing-tools, with just the faintest shadow of a sigh, and devoted herself to soothing and comforting her young patient.

She spent some time in bathing and rubbing the "place that ached," as Ranney called it; then put on a comfortable little wrapper, which Aunt Mildred had found strength to make for

him, and took him on her lap by a front window, that he might be diverted by what was
passing, as well as by the story she was telling
him.

Suddenly Ranney sprang up, exclaiming joy-
fully, "There he comes! I didn't s'pose he
would!"

"There *who* comes?" said Eunice. "See
here, little man! If you jump around in that
style, I shall have to bathe you again!—Who
is coming?"

"Why, Roland! He said he would.

"See! He's been to that house opposite,
but I know he meant to come here! Yes, now
they've told him, and he is coming across!"

"Why did you not tell me before that he
was coming, you little rogue?" cried Eunice,
hastily putting Ranney in trim to go down-
stairs.

The child forgot his aches in the pleasure of
greeting Roland, and Eunice was quite as
much pleased to see him, though wholly taken
by surprise.

"Ranney has been expecting you, it seems;

but he had not told me you were coming here;—pray how did it happen?"

"I only told him that I might possibly come to Holmeford," said Roland: "it was not settled when he left.

"Father was partly expecting to come on here, on business; and he had promised, if he did so, to let me accompany him, as the business was partly on my account."

Eunice looked the question which she did not ask; and to which Roland replied, smiling:

"Father thinks I need a year at some first-rate school, to finish fitting for college; and Dr. Barnwell's has been recommended to him,—a little out of Holmeford, you know, just far enough to have country privileges.

"We are to go out there, to see Dr. Barnwell to-morrow, so I thought I would find you out to-day, for I wanted very much to see you, and Ranney."

A lively conversation followed. Roland had to tell all the Mansfield news, and to answer Ranney's eager questions. The little lad felt as if he had been away from home almost as long as Eunice.

"And how have you got on with Mr. Hale this winter?" Eunice asked.

"Oh, do you not know that Mr. Hale left, some weeks ago? He had a much better offer than the trustees could make him, in Mansfield.

"We have had a lady teacher since, but I do not think she will stay, permanently: the Academy will be all ready for you to take, Eunice, when you want it."

Eunice smiled; and Roland added:

"You have been sadly hindered in your studies this winter, haven't you?—I was *so* sorry to hear about your eyes."

"Yes, but it was not *all* lost time: uncle was so kind, and took so much pains, that I think I have improved faster than would be supposed."

"Improved in more ways than one!" was Roland's mental comment, as Eunice arose to speak to her Aunt Edith, whom she heard passing in the hall.

Mrs. Hartwell entered, and gave Roland a warm greeting, and a cordial invitation to stay at her house; but this he was unable to accept.

The young friends and schoolmates compared notes as to progress in their studies; and Roland exclaimed in surprise, when he found how Eunice had got on.

"I don't think you could have accomplished as much at school, *with* eyes!" he said.

Altogether it was a very pleasant incident,— this visit; and Eunice concluded, after Roland had gone, that it was just as well that she was detained from her lesson, that day.

CHAPTER XV.

Pleasant Things.

"He wills His people to be glad,
  Sin only can their peace destroy :—
He never made thee to be sad,
  Who gave thee such a heart for joy."

"ARE you very tired, Ranney?"

"Yes!" The answer was accompanied with the weary sigh which meant "*More* than tired!"

Eunice laid down her book, and seated herself in a low chair.

"Come, dear, let us rock a little while, and it will soon be time to go to rest."

It was just after dinner, and Cousin Dick was in the room. Ranney looked a little shy, as if fearing to be laughed at if he let his sister hold him. But indeed the slight little figure was no heavy burden;—though his friends hoped that he gained a little, on the whole, the improvement was not perceptible in his outward appearance.

Cousin Dick felt too sorry and anxious for him to have any disposition to tease.

He lifted him lightly upon his sister's lap :— "That's a capital way to rest, isn't it, Ranney?" said he : "I wish I had a sister to pet *me*, when I have a headache!"

"What were you reading, Pussy? shall I read aloud to you?"

"Thank you, Cousin Dick; I was only looking out the Collect, and so on, for to-morrow."

"The Fourth Sunday after Easter," said he : "I shall like to read it, too." And he opened the Prayer-book, and read the Collect reverently.

"'O Almighty God, who alone canst order the unruly wills and affections of sinful men ; Grant unto Thy people, that they may love the things which Thou commandest, and desire that which Thou dost promise ; that so, among the sundry and manifold changes of the world, our hearts may surely there be fixed where true joys are to be found : through Jesus Christ our Lord."

He seemed struck with the words, and held the book musingly in his hand. Presently, meeting a glance from Eunice, he said :

"It *is* appropriate, is it not, little cousin, for one who is just beginning to wish that his unruly will and affections may be thus ordered?"

"It is appropriate for every one of us," said Eunice, with a thrill of hope and pleasure;— "but, oh, Cousin Dick! I am so glad!"

"So glad of what?" he asked, quietly.

"That you have decided;—that you will be confirmed!"

"I have not said that, coz."

"But I know you will!" replied Eunice, looking up at him with a happy smile.

Dick did not answer, but she knew that he was not displeased.

"Shall I read on?" he said; and read the Epistle, and the Gospel for the day.

"He will guide you into all truth," he repeated, thoughtfully:—"if we might only experience that to be true, Eunice."

"But it is!—I mean, we shall be sure to find it so, Cousin Dick, if we will *let* ourselves be guided,—or submit to be 'ordered,' as the Collect says."

The young man gazed thoughtfully into her earnest face.

"The 'ordering' is not always as we should choose for ourselves; is it, Eunie?"

For all answer, Eunice reached a hymn-book from the table, and turned readily to one which had of late become a favorite with her:—the now well-known hymn commencing:

"Lead, kindly Light."

She handed the book to him, pointing to this, with a smile.

"Is the Bishop coming to the church to-morrow?" asked Ranney.

"Yes, dear."

"I wish *I* could go to church! I do want to, so much."

"Be patient, dear little man, and I hope you will soon be able to go again;—but you could not bear it now; you would get too tired."

"I know what the Bishop said, when Roland

Wells, and the others, were confirmed:—he said:

" 'Defend, O Lord, this Thy child with Thy heavenly grace!'

"I wish I were old enough to have the Bishop put his hands on *my* head!"

Eunice glanced timidly at her cousin, who sat, an interested listener, and awaited her reply.

"You will soon be old enough, darling!— But you remember *Who* placed His hands on *little* children, and blessed them?"

"Yes, Jesus!" said the child:

"I wish that His hands had been placed on *my* head,
That His arm had been thrown around me,"

he added, quoting from his little hymn; but the words startled Dick, who was not familiar with them.

"But you know," rejoined his sister, that hymn says, too:

" 'But still to His footstool in prayer I may go,
And ask for a share in His love!' "

Ranney nodded, understandingly.

He seemed unusually bright, the next morning, and it was a lovely day.

Cousin Dick held a whispered consultation with Mrs. Hartwell and Eunice, the result of which was a decision that Ranney might go to church.

Dick offered to wheel him thither, himself, and to bring him home again.

The child seemed so greatly to enjoy the service, and to appreciate the privilege of being again at church, that his friends felt it would be safe to repeat the experiment, at another day.

And did Eunice enjoy the service?

She did, indeed!

Glancing towards her uncle's pew, from her seat with the choir, she met the eye of her little brother, beaming with pleasure, as he nestled beside his aunt; and saw her cousin Dick also, evidently prepared to enter reverently and heartily into the solemn services of the day.

The low tones of the organ recalled her attention to her own duty; and a pleasant and blessed duty it seemed, that day!

As the candidates for confirmation were summoned to the chancel, Eunice felt her hand

clasped meaningly in that of her friend, Miss
Lynde.

Dick North was among the number ; and the
four young girls, her classmates in Sunday-
school, and others whom they knew, and in
whom they were both interested.

They followed them in the reception of the
holy rite, with heartfelt sympathy and prayer.

That week was to bring Eunice a joyful surprise. She was returning with Ranney from
Miss Lynde's, one day, having been practising
with her, as usual.

As she drew near home, a carriage from the
depot drove up in front of the house, and a
gentleman alighted, who, as Eunice thought
at the little distance, looked wonderfully like
her uncle himself.

But who could be with him? She had not
heard of any expected guests.

Certain mysterious observations which had
passed at breakfast that morning flashed
through her mind, and made her quicken her
pace, just as Ranney shouted in great excitement :

"Eunice, see! There is papa! Yes, and mamma too! Oh, *please* hurry!"

This request was not needed. The perambulator flew along the walk, and in another moment Eunice was fondly clasped in her mother's arms.

Such a long embrace it was, that her father at length smilingly asked: "Have you not a kiss for me too, my daughter?"

Then followed a torrent of questions and exclamations, which could not well be transcribed.

As it proved, the visit had been rather suddenly resolved upon, in compliance with repeated and urgent invitations from Mr. and Mrs. Hartwell; the latter had received word that they were coming, the evening before, but had concluded to let it be a surprise to Eunice and Ranney, as indeed it was.

"And what did you do with all the children?" inquired Eunice, in a puzzled tone.

"The little girls and George are with Mrs. Wells, who kindly offered to take care of them if we would come."

A slight tremor in her mother's voice showed Eunice that she was thinking of her infant boy, taken so lately into heavenly guardianship ; and she clasped the dear hand she held with a sympathizing pressure.

One principal inducement to this visit had been that the parents might themselves see Ranney's physician, and obtain careful instructions as to the course best to be pursued with him, when he should return home.

"You will take us home when you go, will you not?" queried Eunice, when allusion was made to this. •

"We thought a little of it, when we left home, dear ; but our friends say 'no!'"

"Leave them here, by all means, another month," said Mr. Hartwell. "It will be then only the middle of June, and they will return before the warmest and most trying weather.

"We think our little city is as pleasant as most country places, at this season!"

"How wonderfully Holmeford has grown and improved, since my last visit here!" remarked Mr. Somers.

"Yes; we have, in fact, become so *cityfied* that I do not know as you will find your daughter contented with rural life again!"

Eunice smiled : and Mr. Somers rejoined in the same playful tone : "You cannot tell what Mansfield may aspire to be, in the course of a few years; it may rival Holmeford! But really," he added, "joking apart, the proposed railroad will make a great difference with our place."

This conversation was at dinner-time. Cousin Dick caught the last remark, and followed it up with sundry interested inquiries.

Eunice wondered a little that he should seem so much concerned in the progress of Mansfield; but as the ladies were engaged upon topics of more immediate interest to her, she did not hear all that was said.

Mr. and Mrs. Somers remained a whole week in Holmeford, although they at first thought they could stay but two days.

It was a delightful week to Eunice. It was so nice to have her mother become acquainted with dear gentle Aunt Mildred, whom she had

never met before;—and with her darling Miss
Lynde.

Mrs. Somers went also with Eunice one day
to see Mrs. Merritt, who was quite indisposed at
the time, and unable to be out.

Eunice said 'she *did* want her mother to
know Rhoda's mother!' and she was not disappointed in the interview.

"Don't you like Cousin Dick, mother dear?"
she asked, one day.

"I do, indeed; I think he is a really esti-
mable young man," was the reply.

"But isn't it odd that he and papa should
take such a mutual liking!" said Eunice.

"There they go, walking out again together!"

"Then you have not noticed the drift of their
conversation?" said her mother:—"I suppose
it is no secret from *you*, although of course you
will not speak of the matter out of the family,
until it is fully settled.

"Cousin Dick thinks seriously of entering
into partnership with your father, in his business."

14

"Oh, mother! Is it possible? How nice that would be! But I thought," she added, "that father's business of late had been hardly sufficient to offer many inducements to a partner!"

"Very true; but you know, my love, he has been crippled by ill-health, and want of means. Our friend Dick has capital to invest, and has been looking around for a good opening, to start for himself. He is well suited with your father's line of business, and seems to put a high value upon his experience and wisdom;— none *too* high, you and I would say! Then you are aware, dear, that the new railroad is fairly commenced and is to be pushed through with all possible expedition; and this, as Dick has foresight enough to perceive, will make a great difference in the business of our town.

"Still, even if they resolve upon the partnership, they will not fully decide to go on at Mansfield, until Dick has been there, to look around with your father. He proposes now to escort you and Ranney home, next month, and see the place for himself."

Eunice clapped her hands in delight.

Mrs. Somers smiled, and said: "Do not be setting your heart too much upon this plan, my darling; you know it may very possibly fall through."

" I will *try* not to, but I'm afraid I cannot help thinking of it!"

She mused a little, and then said:

"I have had some lessons, you know, this winter, about setting my heart too strongly on any plans; but after all, mother, don't you think it is right to look on the bright side, and see all the pleasant things we can?"

"By all means, my darling; and you can understand that to one who has truly committed his way unto the Lord, there is always something to make the heart rejoice, yes, and sing for joy, even in the darkest hours!

"Do you remember those lines in the little poem we were looking over last evening?

> " 'Let thy heart open to the bliss
> He would breathe in at every pore;
> Live but in Him, thou canst not miss
> His mercies in their boundless store.'

" And then again :—

> "'And so this world, in its pure prime,
> Was once an easier way to God.
> But still 'tis glorious, and the path
> Even of its fallen beauty, lies
> Open to love, and clear for faith,
> Step after step, into the skies !'"

Dr. Browne, in his interview with Mr. and Mrs. Somers, gave them considerable encouragement with regard to Ranney.

He thought that with careful management he might escape any tedious chronic disease ; yet he warned them that the child might be delicate and ailing, even with the best of care, for months, perhaps years.

This opinion was much more favorable than their fears had led them to anticipate.

They returned home, at the close of their pleasant visit, relieved and hopeful as to their little boy, and sincerely pleased and thankful for the evident improvement of their eldest child.

Eunice had indeed improved, as Roland had observed, 'in more ways than one,' during her sojourn in Holmeford.

She had grown and strengthened physically; and, although she was not one who would be pronounced handsome, she possessed the charm of expressive features, animated by intelligence, and rendered winning by the gentle loving spirit within.

Yes, the heart of the father and mother rejoiced especially, that their child had perceptibly grown and increased in the knowledge of Christ Jesus our Lord.

Dearly would her intellectual advantages have been purchased, in the estimation of these faithful Christian parents, had she failed to make progress in heavenly wisdom;—had the influences of her winter's home blighted, or stunted the growth of that plant of the Lord's planting which they had so devotedly nurtured; —the character of a disciple of Christ!

CHAPTER XVI.

"Sweet Counsel."

"No dream :—but an abiding consciousness
Of an approving God ; a righteous aim ;—
An Arm outstretched to guide them, and to bless!"

HE visit of the parents of Eunice had given much pleasure to all the household, as well as to Eunice and little Ranney.

"I shall expect more of you, my dear," said Miss Dora, in her lively way, "now that I have seen your parents. You ought to be a pretty good girl, with such a mother !"

Eunice thought so too.

The days sped rapidly, more so than ever, now that the time was fixed for her return home. There was so much that she would like to do before leaving Holmeford.

(214)

Ranney was not particularly better; but Aunt Mildred was.

She was very fond of the child, and liked to have him with her; and he was very happy in her room.

"Don't trouble yourself about Ranney, when he is with me, my dear;" said the kind old lady, when Eunice looked in, one morning, thinking she might be wearied of her young visitor.

"Let him stay here as much as he likes, unless it is time for some medicine, or nursing. I know you can make use of all your time, in these busy days."

Eunice saw very little of her cousin Dick, who seemed unusually occupied; though he found time for an occasional allusion to 'the famous time' he and Ranney would have, when he took his vacation, and went home to Mansfield with them.

The passing seasons of the Church were not unnoticed, amid the eager claims of earthly work.

On Monday of Whitsun-week, Eunice had

proposed to take Ranney to church, with the aid of the friendly wheels which had been such a help to her;—and then, after service, to go to Miss Lynde's to practise.

The morning proved rainy, and consequently she was expecting to give up going, but Mrs. Hartwell interposed.

"My sore throat will prevent me from going out, but I can attend to our boy, and you can go, Eunice.

"You need not hasten home, either. I expect Ranney will be very much amused with the paint-box which Dick brought for him, Saturday night. Ah, I forgot to mention it to you!—I thought it would come in play for just such a time : so you can practise as long as *your* throat will bear it :—I am glad *mine* is not to be tired in that way this morning!"

"I wish every part of me were as tough as my throat!" cried Eunice, gayly ; "I think that is made of gutta-percha ; it never tires! But auntie, I am very much obliged to you for letting me go. I will try to make good use of my morning.

"How kind Cousin Dick was to think of a paint-box for Ranney! I will cut out some pictures from those pictorial 'Weeklies,' in the library, if you have done with them, before I go; and show him how to color them."

Ranney was delighted with his new employment, and Eunice left him seated at a table with his coloring apparatus before him, happy as a king.

"I suppose we are not to have many more of these pleasant singing hours, Eunie!" said Miss Lynde, when there was a pause in their practising.

"No; but they have given me something to remember you by, as long as I live;—though I never could forget my darling teacher!—It is *so* nice to be able to read music, and sing by note; and I really am not afraid to try a new tune now!

"How I *wish* I could do something to show how much I thank you for all the pains you have taken to teach me!"

"Why, my dear child, I have been 'thanked' and rewarded all along! "I have only one further reward to crave, and that I need hardly ask ! "

" What is it? " inquired Eunice, eagerly.

" That this talent, which I have been permitted to aid in developing, may ever be consecrated."

Perceiving that Eunice looked a little awed and perplexed, she hastened to add :

" I mean, darling, that in the first place, you will always be ready to serve God with your voice, as for instance you have had opportunity to do already, this spring."

" It seems to me now that I shall always be glad to do *that !*" said Eunice.—" I wonder if I can help at all in our choir at home?

" Now I think of it, mother mentioned that one lady who used to sing has married and left town. Perhaps I *shall* find work there !"

" And from your buoyant tone, dearie, I see that you deem it *pleasant* work.

" So it is, and a great privilege : and yet you may meet some trying things in it :—you may hear unpleasant, or perhaps even unkind criticisms upon your singing, when you have been humbly trying to do your best, and when you are conscious that you are supplying a place which might else be unfilled.

"I speak of these things only to warn you, darling, in case God gives you this work to do, to remember that it is in His service, and for Him; and that will help you to be patient, and not easily provoked."

"I *will* try to remember, dear Miss Lynde! But you said, 'In the first place;' how else can I consecrate my voice?"

"By resolving never to sing any profane or irreverent words; or any sentiment which you would feel ashamed to avow, in any other form."

"I hope I should not do *that;*" said Eunice.

"You look a little shocked, dear; but indeed, we need to be a little on the watch in this matter: very strange and unseemly words are often uttered, unthinkingly, disguised by some popular or pleasing air!"

"I believe," said Eunice, after a pause, "my singing lessons may prove more useful to me than my drawing: although I have enjoyed that *so* much, when I could go on with it! But I'm afraid what I have learned will be pretty much a loss, for I cannot do much yet without a teacher, and I don't know when I shall ever be *taught* any further; — sometimes I think it was not wise to begin!"

"Then you think wrongly, my dear! It was right and wise to use the opportunity as long as it was given you. You cannot tell of how much use the knowledge you have now gained may be to you, if you should never be able to learn more of the art.

"When I was a little girl I went to school to a lady who was very ingenious at different kinds of work.

"She always kept some bit of light work in the drawer of her table, in the school-room, to take up at recess, or when she had a spare moment or two.

"I remember once standing by her, watching her busy fingers at a piece of netting, which looked like puzzle-work to me.

"I said something to this effect: that 'I

should like to know how to do that, if I could ever make it of any use.'

" 'I shall be very glad to show you, some time,' said my teacher; 'and as to making use of it, do you always make a point to learn *everything worth knowing,* as you have opportunity; and it will be sure to come in play, in some way.'

"I have very often proved the truth of this saying of my old teacher. So do not quarrel with your drawing-lessons, Miss Eunice."

Eunice smiled. "I suspect," she said, "that I set out with too magnificent plans and desires, and so I feel disappointed, when they come to mind.

"And I am *always* doing that same thing, Miss Lynde.

"I do *wish*—that is, I think it would be such a *comfort* if we could know just what we had before us, to do, in our lives ; and then perhaps we should not make so many mistakes, and *try at* so many things that we can never succeed with."

"Stop, stop, my dear girl! You are on the wrong track entirely!

"Do not wish that we could see before us in the path of life; we are far happier as we are;—our Father 'knoweth the way that we take;' 'Our times are in His hand.'

"And as to *trying at* so many things that seem of no use;—that reminds me of school-days again.

"Think how many of our tasks, as little children, seem to us of no possible use; how often we have heard some sturdy little fellow mutter, 'What's the good of learning this!' Yet all the while, his intellectual powers were being developed and disciplined to grapple with future difficulties, and remove obstacles in his onward career.

"It is just so, very often, darling, with those things that we regard as mistakes,—a waste of time and effort. Often we live to see the good that has come to us through these very means; and if we cannot see, we 'know that all things work together for good to them that love God;'—even their failures."

Eunice mused a little over these words.

"I know what you mean, Miss Lynde; but

we ought to look forward, and plan, and try to do what is for the best; shouldn't we?"

"Think over the Collect which we use this week, dear, and it will answer you.

"Yes; we are taught to pray that we may 'have a right judgment in all things.'

"But we also pray that the same blessed Spirit who alone can guide us, will cause us 'evermore to rejoice in His holy comfort,' whether our plans seem to us to succeed, or to fail."

"Our Collects always give us something to think about," responded Eunice.

"And you have helped me *so* much in using them. Dear Miss Lynde, how I shall miss you!"

"Call me *Frances* now, Eunice; you and I are to be always friends, you know," said her companion, drawing her more closely to her side.—"And,—you may not *always* miss me!"

Eunice looked up suddenly, and catching the significant look and smile which accompanied these words, a whole train of delightful possibilities rushed across her mind.

"No, no," said her friend, laughingly, placing her hand on her lips as Eunice was about to interrogate her:

"I shall not explain my rash announcement, so you need ask no questions, now. Wait patiently a little longer, my dear."

"Well, but you cannot keep me from *guessing*," replied Eunice, mischievously. "Oh, if things should come out as I *hope*, it would be almost *too* nice!"

And Eunice tripped homeward that morning with a light step, a happy heart, and a mind full of useful and helpful thoughts.

CHAPTER XVII.

Home Again.

" Love all on earth that charms thee so
With a whole heart; 'tis life to love,
But still remember, life below
Is but the school of Life Above!"

THE middle of June, the time appointed for the return, was now at hand.

Mr. Neville, in parting with his pupil, gave her many useful directions for improving herself at home in drawing; and warmly expressed the hope that he should have the pleasure of instructing her again, before very long.

The packing up was rather a different matter from that when Eunice left home. Aunt Dora, under pretext of "giving her dear girl all the time possible for her studies, now that her eyes were better," had taken charge of her spring

15 (225)

outfit, aided and abetted by generous Aunt
Mildred ; and it was found necessary to replace
the little old-fashioned hair trunk with one much
more capacious, to be returned by Cousin Dick.

Eunice spent an hour or two of her last afternoon in Holmeford with Aunt Mildred.

She was unable to sit up that day, but re-
clined on her lounge, and Eunice sat on a low
seat beside her, holding her hand in both her
own.

Both felt that it might be their last opportunity for " a good talk," as Aunt Mildred termed
it.

" I hardly think I shall tarry here until you
come again to Holmeford, my darling," she
said ; " but you will not forget the old auntie
who loved you very much, will you?"

Eunice kissed her fondly, with tears in her
eyes, for answer.

" We shall meet again, dear child, in our
Father's House ; and then we shall recount the
mercies of these days with thankful hearts, and
praise Him who led us to be ' helpers of each
other's joy.' "

"I think that help has been all on one side, dear Aunt Mildred!" Eunice said, smiling through her tears: "you have been doing something to make me happy continually, since I came here."

"And you have been a great comfort to me, my love!

"But Aunt Edith is calling; I must not keep you any longer now; you will come in to-morrow to say 'Good-bye!'"

It was rather a hard task to say good-bye, when the time came; for Eunice had reason to feel warmly and gratefully attached to her Holmeford friends.

They had a pleasant journey home; Cousin Dick was exceedingly kind, making Ranney as comfortable as possible, and causing the time to pass very agreeably to Eunice.

Dick was lively as ever, but his conversation had lost the flippant tone which had once struck Eunice unpleasantly. The two had now many subjects in common, of real interest; and Dick no longer regarded his cousin as a child, to be teased and bantered for his amusement.

At home once more! And how delightful it was to be again in the midst of the dear circle.

The dear little place was looking its very prettiest; so in fact was Mansfield in general; and Dick was quite charmed with his proposed place of residence.

He and Mr. Somers were together most of the time, during his stay, talking up their mutual plans.

Eunice was delighted to see that her father appeared in better health than she had seen him in a long time; and he was evidently encouraged and hopeful as to business prospects.

At the tea-table, the evening before Dick was to return to Holmeford, the announcement was made that all was arranged, for the new partnership, to go into effect in the early autumn.

The boys received the tidings with a shout of joy, excusable under the circumstances; George, as well as Ranney, having found out that Cousin Dick was "tip-top," as they expressed themselves;—" the nicest sort of a fellow for a grown-up cousin!" George added.

Mrs. Somers and Eunice were no less pleased, although more quiet in their demonstrations of joy.

" Are you really coming back to Mansfield to stay, Cousin Dick?" queried Bess: " and will you live with us, and be our cousin all the time?"

"I'll be your cousin, unchangeably, little lady; I'll promise, so far! But as to where I shall live, and how, I am not so certain."

Meeting a merry glance from Eunice, he added:

" I *may* be obliged to consult some one else in making such arrangements."

" Eunice evidently fancies herself in the secret," observed Mrs. Somers: " and I judge from her face that she has no doubt of the arrangements being satisfactory to all concerned."

" I don't know how they may feel on the subject in Holmeford;" said Eunice, "but I am sure *we* shall have reason to rejoice."

Eunice made an early visit to baby Walter's grave, her little sisters leading the way. It was in a lovely spot, and the sister felt that she would do well to visit it often, and thus remind herself of resolves seriously and earnestly made, but which she feared, from past experience, might be too easily broken.

Eunice readily fell into a round of duties, when settled again at home.

Ranney, at her request, remained her especial charge; the little fellow was evidently improving, though slowly; he enjoyed being at home, and with the other children, once more, but when he was feeling poorly, or in pain, he was easily crossed and irritated by the others.

Eunice tried hard to teach him patience and forbearance; she often told him of her friend Rhoda. Ranney was always interested in hearing of her;—and Eunice, while teaching him, humbly endeavored to teach herself also, constantly, by the remembrance of that sweet example.

Eunice did not attempt much in the way of study, for the summer, except an occasional review, occupying a few hours of each week; and some practice at drawing.

But, early in July, Roland returned home. He had been visiting relatives in other places, since his short stay in Holmeford.

He was full of the spirit of study, expecting to enter Dr. Barnwell's school at the beginning of the fall term.

"Suppose, Eunice," said he, when they had one day been talking upon their favorite themes, "suppose we study together, for an hour or two, every day when you can spare the time;— we might read Latin together, and help each other; what do you say?"

"You can very easily arrange to spare the time, I think, daughter;" said Mrs. Somers, to whom Eunice had appealed by a questioning look; "and I think it will be an excellent plan!"

And so it proved; if the satisfaction of the young people was any test.

The little band of singers who led in the church music at Mansfield, gladly welcomed an additional voice, when Eunice modestly offered her aid.

And Eunice found another field of work opened before her.

Talking one day with their venerable rector, and answering his inquiries about Church work in Holmeford, she chanced to allude to the Infant Class of the Sunday-school.

"Ah!" said Mr. Parker, that is something I am very anxious to see started here. There is quite a flock of little ones, of suitable age, in the parish, if I could but find a teacher familiar with the work."

"Eunice, dear," said her mother, after a pause, "did you not gain a little experience, when you were entrusted with Miss Scott's class, for a time? I recollect your aunt mentioned the circumstances, in one of her letters, while you were troubled with your eyes, last winter."

"Indeed! Did you so? Then, my dear, you will be just the one to undertake this work for me.

"And a good strong voice, too! You can

train the little things in singing. My dear
child, do not object ;—I said you might undertake this ' for me,' but you know Who calls you
to it, through me ; and Whom you may serve
in taking up this duty."

" But I am so young, dear Mr. Parker : indeed I should be glad to do it, if it were not
for that."

" You are young, but you had early nurture,
my dear ; and you have some especial qualifi-
cations. Besides, your little scholars will be
young, in proportion ; and you will be all the
time out-growing this objection.

" What say you, then ; shall I gather my little
lambs, and make a beginning next Sunday ?"

And Eunice made answer, as she felt con-
strained to do, to a similar request, before :

" If you think I can do it, sir, I will *try*."

Correspondence with Holmeford was kept
up briskly through the summer.

One letter, received by Eunice from her
friend, Frances Lynde, will furnish some ex-
tracts which may interest the reader.

"Holmeford is very quiet now; in fact, it is too warm for much exertion.

"You ask if I expect to leave town this summer: I think not; as it will probably be my last summer under my father's roof, I do not feel much disposition to roam.

"Yes, Eunie, the time is decided upon; *it* is to be near Christmas;—probably the middle of December. And having honored you with this confidence, I have now a request to make of you.

"I want you to be one of my young brides-maids. I shall have two of my Sunday-school girls besides, I think; but I have set my heart upon having you.

"Consult your dear mother; and in your next letter promise me that you will be here.

"I called at your aunt's, a few days since, and sat awhile with Mrs. Ellett. I think she is a lovely old lady. She spoke very fondly of you, and seemed to miss you very much. I think she has failed since I saw her last.

"Your Aunt Edith spoke of her desire that

you should spend some time with them again this Fall, and perhaps go on again with your drawing.

"Perhaps I should not mention this, but I judged from her manner of speaking that she had already made the proposal :—if you should do so, you might be *on hand* at the time I need your services.

"Dick was delighted with his visit at Mansfield, and is well satisfied with his prospects.

"He is quite desirous that I should see the place ; but I prefer to wait now until I see it as my home ; although I have also your tempting invitation as an inducement, for which many thanks.

"I must not omit to mention that I saw Mrs. Merritt recently. She bears her loss in a truly Christian spirit, although she evidently misses her dear daughter more and more. The next children are boys, you know ; and Rhoda was very much of a companion for her mother, although so young.

"Mr. Robertson inquired after you when I saw him last : indeed many friends here hold you in loving remembrance; but none more truly do so than

    "Your friend,

      "FRANCES LYNDE."

Eunice handed the letter to her mother, and mused, while she was reading it.

This was the first intimation, except in a general way, of her Aunt Edith's intended invitation.

Mrs. Somers gave back the letter, saying quietly:

"Well, dear, what do you think of it?"

"I hardly know, mother; it will require a good deal of thought. I should like very much to be there at the time of the wedding, if you can afford to let me go. But, about the longer stay, there will be so much to consider:— it seems very soon to leave you alone again; and then there is Ranney,—it will depend a good deal upon how he gets on;—and my little class, too."

Some further discussion followed, as was natural; but at length Eunice remarked, laughingly:

"After all, mother darling, auntie has not invited me yet, and many things may happen to hinder the plan. So we need not decide the matter yet."

Mrs. Somers knew that her sister was in earnest in the proposal, and, as matters stood then, it seemed that it would be well for Eunice to accept it; but it was not necessary to say this, and the subject was dropped, for that time. She thought, however, with real gratification, of the different manner in which a similar proposition had been regarded by her child the year before.

Then,—although the difference betrayed itself less by words than by other unmistakable tokens,—all was eager, impetuous desire to enter upon the path which promised so fully to gratify her inclination and ambition.

Now the first question seemed to be, "What is my duty?"—"Lord, what wilt *Thou* have me to do?" and she appeared ready to acquiesce cheerfully in whatever decision should seem to be right.

And here we must take leave of the young

disciple, some of whose life lessons have filled these humble pages.

If any of our readers would fain follow her farther in her course, let them rest content with the assurance, that, having sincerely committed her way unto the Lord, her song, even to the end, will be the same :

" Though here and there some other lot
    Than I had wished befell ;—
  Truth never failed, nor love forgot ;
    All hath been wondrous well !"

www.ingramcontent.com/pod-product-compliance
Lightning Source LLC
Chambersburg PA
CBHW021959050726
47498CB00006BA/1951